SEX, VIC

& t.

WRONG

MOBILITY SCOOTER

\#

Carnality, criminality and uncouth behaviour in genteel, suburban Edinburgh. Plus, online competitions for things you don't need/want can be dangerous in a really bad way…

by Amanda Baker

Copyright

Copyright ©

Amanda Baker

August 2019

The usual blah blah blah

All rights reserved etc.

Chapters

Prologue

1. P.A.N.Ts
2. Is crazy the new normal?
3. Assonant 'amazon' Al
4. Ten seconds from deliverance
5. Premature Pete
6. Frankie needs a pee
7. Delicious, healthy, home-made, gluten-free, veggie sausages
8. Big Bruce
9. The bad idea
10. Stir crazy & charades
11. I blame the parents
12. Carla wants a baby (the sex bit)
13. Nightmare
14. The morning after the night before
15. Getting shot (the violence bit)
16. Bus routes & fate
17. Breaking news
18. What actually happened

Epilogue

Bonus poem – *70's Summer Montage*

Prologue

I joined groovygranz, a granny website I shouldn't have joined then accidentally entered an erroneous competition for an item I didn't need or like or want that got delivered to the incorrect address due to a warehouse side-door confusion and that mix-up led to another not-quite identical but cocaine-packed delivery being brought to my flat where a drugs gang imprisoned and shot me.

Actually, that may be more of a super-speed spoiler than a prologue...

Premature Pete always intended to shoot me. I thought the others knew too, right from the start. It was in his mind, his eyes and every macho fibre of his inadequate self. The last few hours were just a miserable failure of a silly woman to turn the ship around. Pete was the Exxon Valdez (or Deepwater Horizon for younger folk re my analogy of large tankers owned by even larger corporations, covering sea and coastal life with crude oil for endless miserable miles) and I was the random, weathered old seagull about to be rendered flightless by a stranger's colossal mess.

Chpt 1.

P.A.N.Ts

Win a scooter… Win a bloody scooter?

I scanned the newsletter – which I received via email on my laptop because to me email and PCs are still current tech communication and I don't have a smart phone (we'll get to that later). That day's choice of topics on groovygranz was – how to style grey hair – the kind of make-up 'older women' should wear and the disappointing behaviour of politicians. In other words, the sort of chit-chat you might have at a bus stop on a slow day if you were desperate.

Is this it? Win a scooter? Am I supposed to dress in lavender and chiffon scarves with expensively shaped short hair and the kind of clothes that are described as 'stylish' and 'appropriate'? We all know at my age 'stylish' means you didn't buy them at the local supermarket with your wholemeal loaf.

And a scooter.

Not the fun sort the kids use as they hurtle along with abandon towards the park (those that aren't disabled by iPads by the age of 5, foisted on them by their lazy parents) or even to school – which children today seem to actually enjoy up to about the age of 9. No, it's the sort of horrible thing older men and women sit on to glide slowly or rush recklessly along the pavement like a Dalek but with a little more sense of menace and not being wanted. Some people cover them in stickers. I suppose they think that's jaunty. 'Jaunty' is a dreadful word.

OH GOD.

As for make-up – I don't wear it. I know young folk probably think it's a sin at my age not to cover the less than malleable skin but I never got into the habit. Apparently, not wearing full slap these days means a woman is a hero. I read that along with photos of celebrities without the clart, looking seriously into a camera lens like they just invented a new form of cheap, environmentally friendly energy. I was never one of those girls who sit on the train or the bus choking fellow passengers with their beauty chemicals, bringing others closer to their first seizure or – what do you call them… strokes - with their nail varnish fumes in an enclosed space. You want to scream – 'if you want to commit hari-kari by brain poisoning or lack of oxygen, be my guest but why do you have to take everyone else with you, I'm quite looking forward to a cuppa and a bun with my friend Ellen?' But you can't because that wouldn't be nice. And mature women don't behave like that. I'm a mature woman. A granny. I had to wait until my 50s to get to be a granny. My own mum was one in her 40s and her mum at 39 but we won't go into that. I'm fit and healthy but I don't fit and that is a healthy proportion of my problem.

I'm not suggesting women in their 50s should be trying to be 30. Good lord no. Not Liz Hurleying all over the place. I wonder just how much time that woman spends in the gym and the beauty parlour and the hair salon and with the stylist before she does her – oh look I inadvertently happened to be snapped wearing a tiny bikini and a huge hat and dark glasses in very flattering light. Honestly, all the fundraising that goes on you would think someone would have a whip round and buy the old gal some clothes.

Years ago I remember taking my gran out on a sit-on scooter. I thought it would be a doddle and also took my youngest – on her little bike with stabilisers. But my mum's mum was in the habit of being chauffeur driven by the men in her life and had never manoeuvred a car and had no idea about the basics of steering with a steering column. It all ended horribly down a narrow alley with her in the bushes stuck because her 'free' side was side with the amputated leg. I wanted to leave her there and go after my daughter. Someone would have got the old woman out, she made enough fuss and people feel they have to help the elderly.

But the groovygranz site, like all these things kind of sucked me in. They are designed to do that just as computer games are designed to keep youths flicking to the next level and the next until they look down one day and realise they are grown man still wearing boy's shorts and expecting their parents to pay for everything. Gaming, like gambling is designed to be addictive. The makers spend millions of money structuring gambling sites to be highly addictive and then the government makes them slap a little sign on saying gamble responsibly. Sorted.

According to groovygranz, women my age are supposed to have a 'capsule wardrobe' whatever that is. I don't want people telling me what to wear at my age. I thought that stopped when you were 3. Knickers (HUGE/cotton) Bra (NO WIRES) trousers (SERVICABLE/No camel hoof) top – any – comfy. Comfy socks. Comfy shoes. How hard was that? And colours. I don't wear jeans and I don't wear black because I have a personality and life isn't an ongoing funeral. Not yet.

Younger folk get to win holidays or even hampers. Maybe sites for the oldies don't want to include hampers in case you don't have your own teeth. Well – I do. OK they are filled to the depth an Egyptian archaeologist would be happy with but – hey – I got my teeth a bit before fluoride was universal and a lot before grandparents weren't allowed to give you sweets. You can win holidays but not proper ones. Cruises. Floating, festering petri dishes of imprisoned human horror, dumping the waste of millions of captives who produce more effluent because they are bored. If you still have your own un-filled teeth, holidays are supposed to revamp your romance. They show the younger ones strolling along beaches all slim and tanned and obviously going to have sex. Well, if they didn't spend so much time on the internet watching porn (the men) shopping for crap they don't need (the women) they would be more easily – ya know – aroused and less stressed all the time and have more sex without having to travel to the other side of the globe. Good lord – show my guy any bit of flesh at the right time and bob was your uncle – back in the day. Anyhow – he's gone now. If he was still here I wouldn't have been on a site like that anyway. I would have been quickly getting things done, maybe finishing an article that was near the deadline so that I could meet him for coffee and a walk.

I wonder what kind of scooter...

Would it be one of those silly skinny ones that those delicate bird boned women ride – all neat and coiffed and perfectly turned out as if someone put them together once they were actually sitting in the scooter, like a cake topper. They always look straight ahead as if they know it looks faintly menacing in a *Whatever Happened to Baby Jane* kind of way, but they don't care. I have to say that is one of the advantages and liberations of being older. You don't care. At least I don't. On the other hand did I care that much even then? All those things that seemed so important. Yes – I suppose I cared, maybe more than I'd like to admit. Or would it be one of those great big things that look as if they should be on an autobahn pulling a trailer? I once saw a bloke in Newcastle upon Tyne who was so big and on such a massive scooter, I wondered the pavement didn't buckle. More to the point he must have been winched onto it in the way they say Henry VIII was winched onto his horse in his later years. Who knows – maybe killing wives makes you put on weight. Scooter Henry looked like he'd eaten all 6 of his.

If I had a scooter I wonder if I'd be able to make more of a fuss about things instead of always apologising almost for existing. My maternal gran always made a fuss about everything as I've said (Crikey, we haven't got started and I'm already repeating myself.) A fuss and noise. She was a demanding prim donna. Now there is a phrase that is apparently out of vogue. But then being old is out of vogue so no surprise. No one gets old these days. It's becoming against the law. I read an article online (yes – I'm not a complete Luddite) about the increase in venereal disease in the over 50s. It seems the young are having less sex because they are on their mobile phones constantly and getting averse to human contact while the oldies – who are let's face it – the only ones with both money and leisure time – are – to use the vernacular – *getting it on*. I don't have money and I wouldn't say I have leisure time. Leisure time suggests you can do what you want with your time – which in turn suggests the means and wherewithal – but I can organise my own time. I suppose what I am saying in a round-about way is that I don't have and haven't for many years, what my mother still insists on calling a 'proper' job.

So, I ended up on groovygranz because I was researching possible outlets for some new articles I was considering writing. Satire and commentary only take you so far when you've been left behind by technology or you suffer an incapacitating inability to find any of it either interesting or worth having. It puts you so at odds with absolutely everyone it's as if you've gone to live in a cave. I often feel like screaming – 'I didn't choose to live in here' (the cave) you just made it impossible for me to live in the world'. But I don't know who 'you' is unless it's everyone who isn't me. That's possible.

Everyone loves an acronym these days I.M.O and if I had to describe my state I'd say I suffered from P.A.N.Ts – persistent aversion to new technologies.

But the granny site was a revelation. It was a sea of greyness so vast I could almost feel the pull of death. It was a bland land foreign and alien to me, a place of matching slacks and shoes, arch supports and forums about how to deal with thinning hair and husbands with Alzheimer's. Recently I joined one 'stream' and immediately realised I was swimming with the wrong fish. A woman had started on about how she felt she'd 'lost her husband'. I was about to pitch in with an acerbic comment about getting rid of mine a decade and a half ago and thank god. Then I realised she meant because he had one of these old people's illnesses where you forget everything and become aggressive with people close to you. Good job I read further. I don't always. There is another one where you make up limericks and lots about falling out with grown up children and threats of not seeing grandchildren. And people put all this stuff out in public; I got drawn into that myself, embarrassingly. I mean I know young people have no sense of privacy but I thought my generation did. But then I never ever felt part of my generation. What freaks me out more than anything is that 'my generation' especially the women – are now the age of the women who used to look at me as if I was going to eat their livers when I lived in Wrenmouth years ago. A black single parent in a very twee town with as much vibrancy and cultural diversity as a Brexit rally. You'd walk past them in the street. The over-50s. I'd smile – at first. Sometimes The Husband would smile back but never The Wife. She would stare as if I was an exhibit in a freak show and there seemed to be no consciousness that I was seeing her gawp at me. It was much more unsettling than the racist taunts of some of The Youth. But now I am that age. Good lord, if I ever do that to another human being shoot me. Actually don't. I can no longer think of that saying as anything remotely approaching a joke.

So, I was already on and I scanned through stuff. Randomly I clicked on this or that. I noticed an ad for competitions. There was one for jewellery. You didn't have to answer a question or get anything right or even choose an answer from a list or write a review. Those kinds of competitions are few and far between I've noticed. Anything that involves effort is likely to put off 90% of the population. No, all you had to do was input your name and emails address. Presumably you would then for ever after receive email ads for crap you didn't want from the 1000s of companies to whom your details had been passed without your permission. Well to be honest – I'm pretty sure HMRC have a similar racket going or they don't vet their employees very well. I'd never in my life received one of those 'you are owed a tax rebate – send us your bank details' scam emails – until that is – I registered for online tax with HMRC. Coincidence? I think not.

Years ago I did get hit by one of those – change your password now or you'll lose your account - ones. I blush. Not because of the inconvenience to numbers of my friends and acquaintances who were emailed and told that I'd been mugged in a foreign resort and was being held somewhere unsavoury without a passport and they needed to mail money quickly etc. etc. etc. No. It was the knowledge that they would all know I'd been a total idiot. The chances of any of them giving the money was zero – not because I'm a horrible person who they'd be happy to picture languishing in a foreign cell with cockroaches and some oily brutish guards playing cards for turns at sexual violence with me – no – they all know I don't travel abroad so if there had been any doubt that it was a scam that would have nailed it. It was just knowing that all those people – who already had some idea about just how tech-phobic I am – would know I'd been caught by one of the stupidest, least likely to succeed scams then around. More ludicrous even than the plethora of Nigerian princes with banking issues.

BUT

The competition I thought I'd signed up for was the one for the jewellery. Ok – maybe it wasn't the sort of thing I'd wear myself. I'm a pair-of-earrings-if-I-can-be-bothered kinda gal. Maybe a ring if my hands aren't swollen from the heat or I'm not typing – in which case I find it distracting. I used to wear a watch but once on me they wouldn't keep time (!) But – let's be honest – a bit of random, small, inexpensive dress jewellery never fails to come in handy if you look in your diary and see that a birthday has snuck up on you like a sly little street chugger and has its hands out. So I entered what I thought was a competition for some silver jewellery. Nothing showy – it is for 'older women' after all. I barely glanced at the one for the sit on scooter.

Mobility scooters. That is what they call them. That is a misnomer if ever I heard one. They are immobility scooters. Everything that is advertised to make you more mobile immobilises you. Starting with cars. But then I don't understand why people join gyms. That is how out of touch I am. And – no – I'm not an insensitive monster. I know there must be a significant proportion of scooter users who get real benefit out of them, whose lives remain independent because of them. But the others. And the folk like my gran who got one because everyone else had one…

But then I do not understand the majority of labour saving devices. And put those two concepts together 'labour' 'saving' and you have the essence of Western madness in my view. Spend your time and money stocking up on 'labour saving' devices; zip around in an expensive polluting car. THEN join a gym because you need the exercise. Drive out to the country because you need the fresh air. Is anyone else seeing this?

Ferry your kids from door to door then whine because they are still living at home unable to do the minutest task independently. Shove an iPad into your toddlers' hands while he/she is still incontinent and then complain because he/she can't concentrate or think for themselves later.

Don't worry we'll get to the sex and violence very shortly. I'm just setting background and letting you in on some of my foibles as they all play a part.

I don't even see the point of and have never owned either a dish washer or a microwave. I watch my eldest daughter endlessly juggling plates into and out of the dishwasher (after making sure each dish isn't too dirty to go in) and I see the horrible state of crockery and glassware that have survived the vicious and chemical brutality of the dishwasher process and also the fishing out of plates or cups when the balance of not wanting to put the bloody thing on unless it is full is upset by the need to put a meal on the table with said crockery.

I watched in awe once as dinners were set out for two adults and then a do-se-do of in the microwave out of the microwave in the microwave and out of the microwave dance was begun trying to get each meal hot enough. I could have heated up the food in pans on the hob in half the time and the diners wouldn't have had to wait further time for hot-spot pockets of the food to cool from nuclear. Of course the other option is to mix the nuked, plated food about a bit and then serve up what looks like a very large portion of baby slop.

Then I went back to the forum about thinning hair where everyone had been giving medical advice. Maybe you need iron. Maybe you need blood tests. Maybe you need vitamins. There was – in my view – a disproportionate amount of desperate sympathy considering the woman who was – apparently in her mid-60s – had thinning hair not rickets and her entire family hadn't just been wiped out by a tsunami or her crops annihilated by a plague of locusts. Maybe you need to go and take up precious NHS time with your hair issue because no one ever suggested that you get a cut, wear a scarf, stop bleaching/dying/using hair spray 'getting it done once a fortnight at the hairdressers' so it looks stylish to go with your capsule wardrobe. I didn't say that of course. I suggested a trim and a scalp massage. But daft as this woman undoubtedly was, I bet she never entered a competition for a mobility scooter when she thought she was in for a pair of cheap earrings, so who am I calling daft.

If you are not following my background (which is not quite concluded) of how I ended up with a drug-stuffed sit on mobility scooter when I thought I might be getting a pair of earrings that would do for an emergency birthday present then you'd best stop reading here because it doesn't get any more logical.

Chpt 2.

Is crazy the new normal?

Who am I? I don't mean that in a time-to-ask-if-I-know-who the Prime Minister-is way. I mean – in the context of recounting here – who are you dealing with 'dear reader' as Stephen King would say. Get me. Pretensions or what.

I'm nobody and no one. On a good day I'd describe myself as a functioning lunatic, someone who gets by in the world but is often looking around and thinking 'what has all this got to do with me?' I suspect there are more of us out here than the normal people suspect.

Nothing happens here, usually. 'Here' being my life. There is no soap opera and I know from observing and listening that a lot of folk run their lives as if they populate the set of a low budget soap opera from the pat phrases they use to the hysterical, overly dramatic reactions to very basic situations and domestic conflicts. I often wonder how they would cope if anything even vaguely out of the ordinary did occur. Would they be struck dumb, no longer able to scream expletives the way they do over the smallest incident in the street. Would the daily conveyer belt of weepers and wailers and breast-beaters be turned to pillars of salt by the sudden appearance of something genuinely out of the ordinary?

In my own life there would be nothing for you to read-on for if it weren't for the scooter and the shooter. So, in that way it's like any life in the cosy West. In static moments I wonder if I am what would be called in the old days - eccentric. However, in a world where everyone is trying to outdo everyone else for shock value, individuality and uniqueness, nothing short of parking yourself in the middle of the M1 licking the tarmac in front of a Tesco delivery van, humming the theme to *Rising Damp* while farting in time, is going to qualify – and possibly not even then. Will Self agrees so it must be true. I heard him say something similar on Radio 4. I often wish there was a Radio 4 just for me. It would be a channel with magazine programmes and no ads obviously but with better more in-depth news reports and without the ridiculously shallow binary debates and endless suffocation of middle-class white people who have been brought up from an early age to think every utterance that falls from their lips is worthy of attention and who indulge their hobbies and random observations on public radio at the public expense. Plus bloody cricket.

Generally, I can go through days without really speaking to people much and I'm happy with that. NO. I do not mean I am otherwise engaged online interacting with those who have 'liked' my posts or lambasting those who have trolled me. I am not on any social media sites. I mean I literally sometimes don't have reason to interact with other humans. I have managed to make a life for myself where I do not have to go into a physical workplace despite not having multiple online lives like the you-tubers or instagrammers or the – rather old-hat now – facebookers. Not being on such things as WhatsApp means I also avoid the tyranny of group chat – social or family.

It isn't that I do not see the value of these things. Someone I know knew someone who heard of someone locally who lost their dog and after posting a message to that affect with a picture of said mutt, the creature was tracked down and reunited with its ditsy owner. Tadaa. Plus there was a guy locally stealing from churches. Older members of several congregations who are all more IT/social media savvy than me, shared the info on Fb and the police are now able to identify the guy as living in the area and warn others.

But, I have friends who are 'friends' with their kids and kids' friends on Fb. I actually think that is weird and very inappropriate. But it allows them to keep in touch and know what their kids are doing. All I have is the phone and actually going to see them face to face and having to ask them. Do I want to know what they are doing all the time? No. Do they want me to know? No.

Also, I've grown up assuming the world is about to slap me, metaphorically, so I think maybe I brace. People sense it. Albeit not consciously. Or they just feel the difference. The same way you feel the pressure when a storm is brewing even if the meteorological reports are for calm, sunny weather. Now I begin to suspect that if you are the sort of person who braces, the world may respond accordingly and you get what you are anticipating so I now try not to, which can be exhausting.

I'm sure someone with a psychology degree or two ounces of common sense might conclude that growing up in the 1960's/70s non-white in almost exclusively white areas, going to almost exclusively white schools and experiencing those irregular but plentiful moments of rejection and aggression and exclusion that goes with all that jazz may well have influenced my behaviour and attitude to life. All I will say is that I do tend to be drawn to other outsiders and misfits. Not that I want my friends to take offence at that. I know some very normal people too. I'm prone to ridiculous angst and self-doubt. The latter goes with creativity and the former goes with being alive. Everyone is feeling at least a little anxiety right now. It's even a medicalised term which is big pay day for Big Pharma. YES – it's bad living in the UK right now. Politics is the new psychosis. But it's been coming a while and if like me you are sensitive to the air pressure, as previously mentioned, the current shit storm is no surprise.

The only problem with keeping one's distance from the madness with the absence of – among other things – TV, smart phone, car etc. – is that when you do venture into the 'real' world – which looks bloody crazy to me – you are the one left feeling like the mad person. There are real mad people in my family – which is hardly surprising either statistically or considering all factors – but I'm not one of them. And I begin to wonder if there aren't more genuinely mad folk walking around now than ever before. So is crazy the new normal?

In the UK at the time this all occurred – we were at the mercy of what felt like tropical storms. The week before these events, we had torrential rain and a kind of mugginess that was entirely unseasonal for the UK followed by that someone-left-the-oven-door-open heat. But everything feels unseasonal. The world is rocking on its axis and very especially in Britain where we are taking a lead from America in elevating gobshites, charlatans and undesirables to high office.

So, even though the world is going to hell in a handcart and you can only get people to care about the apocalypse if David Attenborough talks about dying polar bears, I am going to tell you my tale which is strange and mundane, odd and commonplace, exhilarating and humdrum. It does not happen on a grand stage or with celebrities – even minor ones. And there is no emotion-rousing music to get you passed any fluctuations in pace, failures of the main actors to be interesting or the plot to hold your attention. But, if you are sitting comfortably, or even if you are not, I will begin.

The story revolves around me, Annie Day-De Freitas or Granny Annie as the grandchildren call me. And I have to say I don't object to being the centre of attention occasionally but under the circumstances I'd have been happy to take a rain check on this adventure.

I live in Edinburgh. And Edinburgh is ok. 'Just ok?' I hear you gasp – a little disgusted. Yes – I know it's famous for Burke and Hare – body snatching and all that. Victorian gothic at its best. It's also famous for the Fringe Festival - but honestly – unless you want wall to wall I've-seen-him-on-the-telly comedians it's not that big a deal any more. There is Princes St with shop doorway sleepers and closed down shops like anywhere else let me tell you. In fact when slimy toad Sir Philip Green had completed the process of 'legally' asset-stripping British Home Stores, the huge store on Princes St was one of the early, ugly casualties. Still-Sir Philip, despite a few whining politicians, took the pensions of people who had worked there for decades and had no idea that the nest eggs they had scraped together by smiling through a thousand trying customers was to be used to fund more yachts. Edinburgh, like a lot of other important cities, bore the obvious scars of his vile greed.

I put 'legally' like that to indicate that I have a much nuanced view of what is legal and what is not. I have always had an old fashioned idea that legality should still have some loose affiliation to morality. Just in the way that money should have some vague connection to value. Neither does. Money is more of a meaningless concept than ever, and let's face it, since it was disconnected from the gold standard it's always been more than tenuous. Our uneven original laws were made by the folk with the power. So, back in history it was the bloke with the biggest stick. Now it's the guys with the biggest offshore accounts and powerful government lobbyists. Or how come ordinary people do time for minor pilfering (which I am not condoning) but the bastards who deliberately wrecked the world economy in 2008 basically got off scot free and were back doing pretty much the same in less than half a decade?

As we are going to be based in Edinburgh for the duration of this account it might be worth pointing out that the term 'scot free' has absolutely nothing to do with wily Scottish men avoiding legal or fiscal reparation. Apparently scot in this context derives from an old Norse term *skot* meaning payment or condition. The English then used the word scot to mean tax. Which if you think about it has a certain irony because the most unfair tax of modern times – the Council Tax – was foisted on Scotland before being rolled out in the rest of the UK.

There is a snobbery here one would usually associate with small towns. Plus, the fur coat and no knickers tone that often characterises places that labour under the need for tourists, is as true here as anywhere. If you are the sort of person who reads angry letters in local papers then you may have seen one last year about the 50 trees that were cut down in the park outside Waverly station to make way for the annual Christmas tourist tat. And Edinburgh cannot afford to lose trees any more than anywhere else. But it is also true – as a good friend once said to me – wherever you go you take yourself with you so that's just my view and 100 different people will see 100 similar things differently. I am fairly sure that the trolley-dragging, phone camera wielding, pavement-hogging men and women who stomp about relentlessly looking at bits of the city through those ever raised lenses see something entirely different to what I see.

You may sense faux cynicism here. You will be saying – well, she chose to live there so it must be alright. And I did and it is. I did not end up here by accident. I chose to live here and have never regretted it. That is what parents say to adopted children. I chose you. You are special. You didn't just land randomly in my lap. And it's true. There is something about making a choice that is special and confers a certain responsibility over and above the mundane.

I am a granny so I shouldn't be the centre of a story at all. I should be a bit part character at most. Female action heroes and, conversely, the kinds of women who always need rescuing are young and beautiful. That is a rigid Hollywood law although things may be changing since producers of good TV series that you can get on DVD have realised that showing older women in key rolls actually doesn't make the viewing public throw up into their popcorn or switch off and watch something else. My youngest daughter was a fan of the early *Walking Dead* episodes which, she tells me, featured female characters 'almost as old' as me. They may not always be exactly model beautiful in books but if the story is translated to the big screen even characters who are described as plain suddenly become 'plain' in a gorgeous Hollywood kind of way. If you read and then saw the film of *One Day* you will know what I mean.

This is just a tale of everyday folk lacking savvy, devoid of self-awareness and suffering low sperm count. I am a mixed-race, slightly mixed up reluctant central character who has to tackle Scottish 'gangsta' Premature Pete, his lush moll Carnal Carla, Big Bruce and li'll Frankie. All while pickling beetroot in my flat in Edinburgh.

And no – although I am black and 'of a certain age' I do not exude tiresome old black mama wisdom or voodoo/hoodoo or staring eyes and premonitions. Nor is there any chicken blood anywhere to be seen. I'm a vegetarian.

In traditional fairy tales young girls have to be motherless to have adventures. These adventures stop abruptly when they are safely married off. God forbid you should have any adventure after marriage. In contemporary fiction and fantasy a woman just needs to be single, young and beautiful with an impossibly toned body. It helps if, at some point, she still needs rescuing even if she started off as the feisty sort. Parents don't come into it. They aren't mentioned unless doing a back story to extend a franchise. Even older male actors have to have a younger sidekick if they are really getting past it and insisting on dragging their old carcases around a film set past retirement age.

So just who the hell do I think I am writing a story about me – a woman for heaven's sake? A woman in her late 50s. Post-menopausal. Pointless. Surely I should be creaking around on porotic bones talking endlessly about my ailments and bothering the GP at least twice a month. If like me you are almost never at the surgery, the up side is when you do go they give you whatever the bloody hell you ask for.

I know this isn't a 1970s beauty contest but I may as well finish telling you some final extra little foibles. I like nothing more than a good clear out – domestic not bowel. You already know I don't go in for modern technology and I have developed a distressing habit of late of yelling at the radio. Also I remember things, which can be terribly inconvenient because when some politician or other is lying it's not a vague sensation it is something I can pinpoint and I always wonder - if I can remember the last time they spoke about such and such and said the complete opposite of what they are saying now – why can't the interviewer. He or she is getting paid. A lot.

I walk for my sanity and one of the local old guys now greets me with a cheery 'hello strider' whenever I pass if he is out doing his garden. I like to walk on my own along paths I know so that I can think and not pay too much attention to where I am walking. By which I mean the route. Obviously you have to pay some attention to where you put your feet or by the time you've been out 15 minutes you'll be knee deep in dog pooh. Or you will have skidded on a bag of turd that someone has left in the path rather than hanging on a bush. I once saw someone sprayed with the stuff because they were passing just as one of those huge, heavy electric bikes (pavement motorcycles) ran over it and it burst like dog faeces Vesuvius.

I like to bake but only because I like to eat cake. I cook well but basic and have a limited repertoire.

I do not have a TV but admit to watching *Come Dine with Me* when at my mum's or anyone else who has a telly – which let's face it is just about everyone. The combination of food, personality disordered people and sarcastic commentary is irresistible.

I would say I love children but I'd only need to follow that with 'and I want world peace' which I do and I'm back sounding like that half-baked teen beauty queen contestant trying to convince the judges they give a G-string about anything other than their weight, their tan and their eye shadow.

I am mixed race which I know is another term that is undergoing scrutiny at present but I am happy with it. My mum is black from the Caribbean – an ex-British salve colony (yum) and my dad was a working class white man who – as far as I know – had never spoken to a black person before meeting my mum. They got married in the 1950s.

My parents did that thing where we'd get called downstairs or in from playing to pay serious attention if there was a black person on the telly. On serious programmes I mean although we loved Floella Benjamin on *Play School*. I did not drag my kids in to listen when black people were on the radio because more often than not they're filling the regular slot where some old white radio presenter gets in a young black representative of 'da youff' to explain in suitable street lingo how they 'escaped gang culture'. Then having listened indulgently and confirmed their entrenched attitudes, the middle class white presenter goes back to the rest of the news – which for the last three years has been nothing but Brexit.

Calling myself a writer is something I am determined to do although I've made more money from renovating properties, selling junk I found on the streets (what a throw-away-world we live in) and informal childminding but I refuse to be defined by where my income comes from. If we do not have self-definition – what do we have? And if I ever doubted the rebellious slave part of my ancestry – there it is.

But whatever went before I am now a woman of later years with no right as far as cultural norms dictate, to the centre of a story of action and adventure, heated passions and danger – albeit that it all the action adventure and danger and sex happens in my very small, unremarkable flat.

This not a tale of yesteryear. What another ridiculous word. It's not a tale of finding love in later life. Been there done that. It isn't a misty eyed story of flashbacks to when I did something interesting in my youth. It's about what occurred a short while ago as the result of clicking the wrong box on my pc. So – let's get on with it.

Chpt 3.

Assonant 'amazon' Al

I have to thank Al for the assonance that allows me to remember his name. Also the assonance that allows me to remember what a total ass he was in all this. And yes, I've used the American 'ass' here to mean the British 'arse' because any aide-memoire at my age is welcome. And anyhow, as a good friend pointed out to me just the other day, if things go on the way they are, in 100 years' time we'll be revolting for independence from America and needing our own 4th of July. I never met Al but found out his name from eavesdropping on the gang.

No, I'm not great with names (rarely forget a face) but amazon Al is easy. I'd never have remembered Fred who worked at the amazon depot or Julian. Do 'Julians' work at warehouses? Or a Ewan. Young Ewan is my dentist. He has a picture on his surgery wall of himself as a dentist which he drew when he was about 6. I find it a little disturbing. But I've never been great with dentists. I suspect that has something to do with the dentist my mum took me to who would not allow parents into the theatre of stainless steel fear and strange smells. He had a nurse who, once the door was secured, had a special hold which involved one hand around a child's wrist with her forearm across the chest so that she could both pin you down securely and hand the instruments of torment to the sweaty dentist. It was important that she secured you firmly as the dentist did not believe in injections before fillings. The problem was you were in pain and you were scared and often it was a struggle to keep breathing through the whole episode so I think I do well to still be attending the dentist of my own volition.

Anyhow, amazon Al the assonating ass was the weak link in the crazy chain. He was the catalyst in the cataclysm that got things going or the spoke in the wheel that made everything go wrong depending on your view.

Amazon Al worked at the local depot where goods arrive and are shipped out in quantities that would make Midas weep – if Midas had ever been interested in unnecessary garden furniture, cheap badly fitting shoes, self-help books, books on carb diets, 'books' about or supposedly 'written by' celebrities or car mounts for mobile phones so that as well as killing us few remaining hapless pedestrians with what comes out of the exhaust, drivers can just kill us with the actual vehicle more regularly. Like the white van driver pulling out of the DIY shop carpark and turning right across traffic a while back with one hand on the wheel of his huge van and the other gripping his smart phone as if he were sitting in the pub rather than in a vehicle capable of taking out a small village. Boy – since this whole thing started, the past may be a different country but even a few weeks back is starting to seem like another world.

Sorry. I'll try to stop emphasising my displeasure by the incorrect use of single speech marks because I know it's lazy. I'm assuming I can predict that you know what I mean rather than explaining myself and if you can't it's kind of pointless telling a story.

So, amazon Al 'worked' at a local depot. (Woops!) Al spent time getting paid at the local delivery depot and he enjoyed it because, with a bit of sneakiness, he could smoke to his heart's content. It didn't take much to content his heart. Plus, he could keep out from under his mum's flat, flaky feet until evening meal time. Meal time was any time because there were no meal times in Al's mum's house. There never had been. That is a subject I won't get into here.

Al gave his mum most of his pay so that she could stay home with her bad leg and order in food while she bought stuff off the telly and Al used his extra little job on the side so that he could afford to smoke weed most of the time.

If you got too near to Al you might mistake him for someone with a particularly bad case of very acidic BO as I did the first time I got close to one of my daughter's school friends whose brother was what they called back then a 'pot head'. I asked my daughter if anyone had ever spoken to the lad in question about his personal hygiene because it was the worst case of BO I'd ever come across. She rolled her eyes —because that is compulsory when you are 16 - and explained the contemporary drug facts of life to me.

Thing is – it's not that I never smelled pot or weed before. I was a student. Yes, a slightly weird one – I mean weirder than the ones who actually make an effort to be weird – in that I never drank alcohol and didn't particularly like parties. And when I was a student, drinking was practically compulsory. But it was only the edgier ones who smoked dope. There would often be a cabal of 'cool' students in the corner of any house party. Some of my friends would be daring enough to sit near the really cool people and reckoned they could feel the effects – which impressed the hell out of me. I wasn't sure I'd be able to differentiate between the effects of being out late, having a dead leg from trying to stand in a cool pose for a very long time while being cold (rather than cool) also a bit bored if the truth were known plus wishing that I actually wanted to be there and 'feeling the effects' of someone else's tiny roll-up which was being shared between a group of 10 people.

Anyhow

I asked my partner about all this (I called him my partner because we never married and by the time we met we were – in my view – far too old to refer to each other as boyfriend and girlfriend) – he had a slightly more interesting youth than me – and he explained it had to do with what the kids were smoking. The stuff I'd caught a whiff of back in the day was daisy dust compared to the highly genetically modified and very brain-burningly strong crap kids smoke today.

Psychosis was just one of the many joys they had to look forward to in early adulthood especially for the little scraps you saw around the streets on a school day who were probably aged about 12 or 13 but looked about 9 because of their awful diets, lack of fresh air and limited exposure to sunlight.

So – amazon Al was one of these. His life was lived in a fog of cheap and horrible dope and the chances of him ever coming down to land from planet Leave-me-alone, were next to zero.

Al was in charge of the x-extra shipments that came and went at the military sized depot through a special, unofficial side door.

Everyone kind of knew and kind of didn't know about the magic side door. By everyone I mean the almost itinerant work force that shifted boxes as per codes and numbers on electronic lists – sometimes by hand and sometimes by electric mini fork lift trucks. There were smoke detectors in the building in order to keep the goods safe. One would assume it was also for the benefit of the people. There were however, no smoke detectors down the side alleys which were littered with the cigarette butts of a thousand future cancer sufferers and just as many psychotic dope heads. None of the regulars had the least interest in doing anything other than getting through the day without getting forked by one of the trucks and claiming their pay.

Amazon Al wasn't the only one with a side door x-extra. I say that because I mean the operation. I do not mean an extra side door. It may be for all I know that lots of folk used the magic side door. But I do get the impression there was only one. It may well have been intended for use by the smokers and it was used by them – but it became a general portal of detritus. Pizzas were delivered there late at night, girlfriends or boyfriends sometimes called there and of course some items that were not strictly on anyone's on-line list and certainly would not have found their way into your basket or wish list also arrived. And some idiot – not amazon Al I hasten to add – no point slandering they guy even if he was an idiot – decided that a good way to deliver cocaine would be in a mobility scooter. Where to store said scooter and move it on? A nice big local warehouse employing a known 'easy-boy'.

So one day when Al actually had responsibility for parking up a legitimate scooter for what should have been a legitimate old lady who probably wore lavender as part of her capsule wardrobe and had her dove grey hair smartly dyed to go with the new dove grey wheels of her new mode of alternative mobility but wasn't, the naughty scooter also arrived. And the naughty scooter ended up not with the delicate, co-ordinated lady because she, whoever she was, was sensible enough not to enter random competitions incorrectly. The wrong scooter ended up with me, because I did accidentally enter the competition and because of side-door complications.

If it is of any interest to you at all the two scooters were not even the same colour. The naughty scooter was maroon and the kosha one was navy blue. And there would have been no sex, no violence, no drugs in my little flat (let's face it – we're only missing the rock and roll) if Al hadn't been so off his face that he couldn't distinguish between a blue and a maroon scooter.

Now – I'm not saying I've never mixed things up. I have put salt into a recipe that required sugar. I've poured milk into the tea caddy instead of the cup. I have done that thing where you send the text to the person you are talking about rather than the person you are talking to about the other person. I know a woman who mistook her husband for a man who loved her rather than a man who was obsessed with himself and just wanted a 'life facilitator'. I've mistaken two steps for the last step and sent myself head over heels in a very undignified way. But this was one spectacular mistake.

You see – everything is coded. Everything is labelled. If the step had had a bright yellow strip on it I might have been ok. If the wrong husband had had a barcode on his forehead which said 'not husband material' my friend might have been ok. But tis our lumps and bumps that make us. Unlike amazon Al, I was able to learn from my mistakes. As Al's brain was pretty much mush by the time he was in his early 20s he was a. far more likely to make dangerous mistakes b. far less likely to ever learn from them.

Assonant 'amazon' Al had already decided he'd have a go on the scooter when it came time to get it from the warehouse onto the van. He didn't even look for the sticker on the front. But he was not the only one looking for fun and others had a go of the scooters; both the scooter which arrived legitimately and was not delivered via the magic side door and the naughty scooter and that is how they got swapped.

A van arrived. And in some ways he too played a minor part. The driver was early because he wanted to finish early and get to his son's parents' evening. He'd never met someone who wasn't happy with an early deliver. The van driver – who already had a partial load, was asking for 'the mobility scooter' and amazon Al was ready for his ride. Weeeeeee. Although he went far slower than many oldies go even when they are on busy pavements next to people with ankles, Al thoroughly enjoyed himself. It was 8am on a Monday morning and all was right with his wee world. Neither Al nor van man made anything of the fact that there was no tag on the scooter. Van man had a list requiring delivery of a scooter and Al gave him a scooter.

A short time later another van driver arrived at the side entrance in a less- road-worthy looking vehicle also asking for a scooter and took the blue one. He'd been expecting a maroon one but there was only one scooter in the warehouse so what you gonna do?

And that is really all there is to say about Al. He is no more than a story stepping stone getting us from one place in the narrative to the next without – hopefully – too much incongruity. No one really cares about characters like Al in stories like these. You will notice I've not even given van man a name. And he could have been a woman but he wasn't. Al has served his purpose.

If I were my gran I'd have invented a whole tedious back-story for Al. I mean, let's face it, he must have started out as a baby same as the rest of us. Prior to his position in life as low grade to-be-pitied off-his-head bit player in someone else's misadventure, he must have emerged the same as you and me squalling into a world of possibilities. Who is to say that if he hadn't had a useless mother he might not have ended up as he did. And I don't mean working in a warehouse. I have friends whose kids have degrees and MAs and even one with a PhD doing jobs you barely need to be able to read for. You certainly don't need to be able to string a grammatically correct sentence together but they have the qualifications and the debt to prove it and they are doing these kinds of jobs. The difference is that Al thinks he is where he was meant to be and in some ways is probably happier. Those others are not where they imagined they'd be when they were getting drunk in fresher's week and thought the world was their oyster.

And what of Al's mum? Al's mum with her bad leg and telly shopping addiction. She used to leave the house. We can deduce this because she had a baby. She must have at least left the house to meet a man to inseminate her. We presume she took Al to school. Maybe he skipped to school full of life and promise and energy just like all the other boys and girls. Perhaps he answered questions, put his little hand up and ran around the playground yelling and shouting with all the others. Perhaps he was the favourite of one of the dinner nannies.

Some kid has to be. Some kid gets extra mash in an ice-cream scoop or the slightly bigger pudding. It could have been Al.

In the early days of school when the keen parents had 'whole class' birthday parties he may have gone to some of those with a wrapped present and anticipation of cake and games and most of the kids too young to have thought about who they ought to mix with. Later when birthday teas were more selective, perhaps he didn't get so many invitations, who knows. Maybe by then mum's relationship had fizzled out and she'd 'let herself go' as they say – more about women than men. Go where I wonder? To the land of varicose veins and telly shopping I hear you reply. To the land where any response to a child's requests or moans or pleas for attention or better food or help with school work are met with 'be quiet' on a good day.

Maybe when Al first started bunking off school with one or two of the other boys, the school rang his mum. Maybe at first she tried to be interested. She certainly never attended any of the school meetings 'about Al'. He drifted around the streets getting his first experiences of how much better life tasted with a couple of mates and a smoke outside the confines of a classroom where he clearly had no business. Al's mum drifted further into a world that was no bigger than the length of the sofa and sometimes a shamble to the kitchen. Mobile phone one side of her immobile body, remote on the other, she delicately brushes crumbs off her redundant bust before clicking to buy the tanzanite bracelet or the opal ring or the bird table or the fairy figurine. She has no money but credit is a wonderful thing. The world is one big Ponzi scheme now where folk who have no money buy stuff with credit and that magically turns *not- money* into *money* for those who already have loads of it. Al's mum has personal debt that would shock the IMF and she barely leaves the living room.

No – all we need to know is that Al was the means by which the wrong scooter got into the right van. We know that the intended recipient found out pretty quickly what had happened because Pete was at my door within a very brief time of the delivery. Maybe someone staked out the warehouse and followed the van or maybe someone made a call to Al shortly after the mistake and Al was able to tell them where the van was going. If I had to choose between those scenarios I'd bet on the former. But I don't bet. Methodist.

Maybe Al got beaten up for his mistake – but maybe not, having him in that position was kind of handy and he really couldn't afford to lose any more brain cells. Whoever dealt with him knew his disposition. They must have anticipated something like this – and so we are back to my guess – a stake out of the premises. Also – stake out really rings true in this type of tale.

Al may be dead, if we are going to uselessly speculate. He may not have died as a result of drug related violence but an aneurism – they are quite popular in stories these days because they happen suddenly and the author doesn't have to think of an explanation for an abrupt but convenient death. Maybe he was so malnourished that his heart gave out.

Maybe Al cleaned up his act and is now running the country. Lots of MP's these days seem to like to confess to 'trying drugs' in their youth. It's all the rage. But Al didn't go to a top boarding school so the chances of his drug taking being forgiven and forgotten and relegated to anecdotes at dinner parties are pretty damn limited I would say.

Thing is, dead or not, Al is now out of this story so in literary terms he is dead and you can stop worrying about him. If you were.

Chpt 4.

Ten seconds from deliverance

I nearly didn't answer the door.

I'd just finished pickling the latest batch of beetroot from my friend's allotment when my morning was disturbed by unexpected, loud knocking on the front door.

I love pickled beetroot. Who doesn't? Lots of folk, but if you boil the beets yourself so they are still a bit firm before adding the Sarsen's they turn out really well. Four jars ready for scoffing later. One for the kitchen cupboard and the rest in the shed. Like many people, my friend has put a lot of his actual garden under concrete. The crematorium look is all the rage as a result – in my view – of all the home-improvement programmes. Grass is really not very fashionable. But he does drive regularly to his allotment to plant veg. Beetroot is one of his big successes.

It wasn't the time they said it would be delivered and I wasn't expecting anyone or anything else. It was, I concluded, probably someone wanting to sell something to me that I didn't want – or more likely these days – get me signed up to the never ending drip, drip of direct debit to pay the flight and accommodation of some shrill charity administrator fulfilling the saviour fantasy they've had since they first saw a starving African child on the telly at the age of 8. The sort who somehow managed to by-pass the information that all these countries would be a lot better off if they'd never seen a white person and would be less economically ham-strung if they were growing crops to feed their families rather than coffee and flowers to sell in UK supermarkets. But by the time I'd had those thoughts the visitor was still knocking enthusiastically so I thought I'd better go.

That's when I wondered if maybe it was the scooter after all; the scooter that should have been delivered in the late morning 'window' not the early one. Sometimes they got those things wrong. And sometimes the so-called window was all day.

The person now hammering at my *door* was in the wrong *window*.

It doesn't take much to make me smile even if I am just talking to myself and that did it which is the real reason I opened the door – about 10 seconds before the guy might otherwise have headed back in the van with the wrong scooter and I'd never even have known how close I came to catastrophe.

Unlike with Al, I never found out the van driver's name.

What would have happened if I'd not gone to the door or even if I'd not been in? Would the driver have come back later? Would he maybe have been set upon as I was but in a layby somewhere while having a break?

That is irrelevant because I did go to the door – a bit miffed but also amused to see the scooter I hadn't intended to enter a competition for. The scooter that should have been a pair of earrings or nothing at all if I'd not been mucking about on the internet. I won't say bored. I rarely get bored and I don't understand those who do.

So, I opened the door to a youngish, pleasant looking man with one of those electronic devices you sign with your finger producing a scrawl which always looks like it was made by a drunken octopus. I never want to touch those things – they are smaller versions of the screens you are made to use to sign yourself in at the GP now – just a flat surface of excrement and urine and nose pickings from all the disgusting people who have touched it before you. I bet Alexander Fleming never envisaged that penicillin would make humans so unbelievably apathetic when it comes to hygiene.

What I do recall about the delivery driver was his aren't-you-lucky smile. As if the delivery of a maroon mobility scooter was like getting a gigantic bouquet of flowers. Having said that, who likes cut flowers with their associations of late I'd better- get-something birthday offerings or something delivered – also in a van - the day after a wedding anniversary – the size and showiness of the bouquet in direct proportion to the lateness. And then you have to stick the bloody things in a vase when what you really wanted to do was put them directly into the bin. I like to see flowers growing in the ground, preferably meadow flowers, not huge gaudy testaments to couldn't-be-bothered. How many mothers have had to spend how many days gawping at garish bouquets and suffocating in the heady musk of shop flowers from son's they haven't seen in six months? But equally, why would anyone welcome the delivery of a mobility scooter and all that it suggests?

Bizarrely, where to put it was a thing I had not considered. But then it was going on Gumtree as soon as I could get that sorted. In the end I got the chap to manoeuvre it around the side of the building to the lean-to / sort of garage/glorified shed at the back of the flat. I've often wondered if it was supposed to be some sort of greenhouse extension originally. It was more the style of a garage and you access it internally through the kitchen but there is no way to ever have got a car around there so it remains a mystery. Maybe the previous owner just liked 'building on' as some folk do and given half a chance there would have been a warren of badly constructed add-ons stretching out into the back garden – which is – thankfully – far more extensive than flats usually have – if at all.

Van man managed to squeeze the thing through the side door – which is slightly wider than a normal door but not as big as garage door. He guided it between some gardening tools, my old bicycle, the buggy I keep for my grandkids and various items that have worn out their welcome in the flat but have not yet found their way to the charity shop or the tip or the bin or the recycle category.

Without any sense of having 'won' something, I regarded the scooter and if you asked me I'd say it looked right back.

It didn't appear very stable and the seat was more of a lumpy perch. Thinking of the state of the pavements around here I wouldn't want to risk it. It's not like we live in an area frequented by tourists where they still have proper paving slabs. It's the cheapest of cheap tarmac around here. I remember an altercation with a rather unpleasant Virgin van driver as he thumped up onto the pavement in front of me and drove along half on half off for about 20 yards clearly looking for his destination address. As I pulled up beside him and he got out looking around at house numbers – I pointed out to him quietly and politely – I am always calm and polite but it doesn't help – that he was a. breaking the highway code b. mashing up the cheap pavement tarmac that had only just been redone because of all the gullies and dips and ankle breaking divots caused by vans, cars and lorries parking/driving along the pavements. I got the predicted mouthful and an assertion that he had every right to park on the pavement – he ignored the driving on the pavement element. He was vile. They always are when they know they are in the wrong. They do not want that pointed out by a woman, especially a black woman with no make-up.

So about two weeks after they (the council or the council sub-contractors or the sub-contractors' mate's Hungarian slave labourers) had finished slapping cheap tarmac around, it was back to normal – in other words anyone even vaguely unsteady on their feet was risking their bones if they actually tried to walk anywhere.

Anyhow – that was ok. I was not in danger of being tipped off the thing. Nor was I going to run the soft grey wheels through any of the dinosaur piles of dog crap that are an every-6-feet feature of most residential areas around here these days. Unless – that is – you are like some of the bright sparks who drag their mutts into the middle of the road – allow them to shit there and leave it. I presume that must be on the assumption that no one ever crosses a road on foot or with a buggy or wheelchair and passing cars will deal with the toxic piles on their behalf – spraying it up into cyclists' faces probably. At least that gets the cyclists back.

I wondered if the grey wheels are to go with all the dove-grey and lavender that older women are encouraged to wear. Would it go with their 'capsule' wardrobes? Would blue not have been better…

After van man had departed with a cheery wave, I noticed that it had a small trunk – like the ones you used to get on those lovely metal tricycles when I was a child. A sort of bin on its side with a curved lid and a fastener. That was the only thing about it that charmed me. I disliked everything else. I disliked what it stood for – which was of course – not standing. I hated the twee-ness of it even the colour. I despised myself for putting my details in the wrong box and proving to myself yet again that I am a fool and should not go within 10 yards of any online site that is not about purchasing a criminally expensive train ticket or replenishing my essential stock of unbleached coffee filtres.

So, in case you are losing track. I answered the door, signed the filthy screen, the van guy brought the scooter around to the shed/garage/lean-to/not-a-greenhouse. I looked at it, it looked at me. The van driver departed at some point I don't recall, pulling the door behind him. I'd met him in the lean-to having entered by the adjoining kitchen door.

Then, as it was the only thing of anything about the scooter that attracted me, I squeezed around the back, scraping my calf on a low shelf holding camping gear and unhooked the lid fixing. I was not, of course, expecting to find anything inside. Why then did you open it you may ask? Why indeed. But would my not opening it have made any difference at all to subsequent events once the thing had been delivered and parked on my premises? I don't know. And I am no Pandora. I really am not. I may well not have opened the little metal boot if it hadn't been for the happy, childish association.

Unlike many women my age, I am remarkably incurious. I am interested in current affairs but couldn't give less of a fig about who is having their driveway done, who ate what or said what and I could never have one of those conversations that are all speculation and assumption about someone else's life. I've known my old gran – on observing someone having work done on a neighbouring house – to invent an entire soap opera to accompany the whys and wherefores of the work – maybe an imminent divorce led to them wanting to upgrade the house for sale – why are they getting divorced? Maybe he's homosexual – she's seen him in far from masculine attire – and on and on until you want to weep and see if some form of new science has found a way for you to reclaim those minutes and hours of your life that someone else aggressively appropriated because you were too polite to tell them to shut up unless they could fill the air with something other than random sound.

Ditto those women and men on the train who – after they've started their stag do / hen do drinking at 10 am, think they are the only people ever to have used the F word so that what everyone else on the train wants is to hear it over and over again. And I am not averse to some appropriate expletives but it is just so boring because there is nothing in-between. It is just verbal offal being punctuated with the F word. Oh – yes – I did say I didn't get bored and there I go saying something is boring. Oh well.

One of the few interesting conversations I ever heard on a train – I mean one which really caught my attention – was two young women talking about how important and stressful their jobs were. Woman1 was an events manager and often had to get lots of people in the same room – often at the same time – to listen to another person saying stuff. Woman 2 worked at – I surmised – an exclusive expensive gym in London. OK, I know 'exclusive gym' is like saying a-la-carte chicken nuggets but stay with me. Woman2 really piqued my interest when she asked woman1 her advice on something the gym boss had requested. The request was to find a way to get the non-perfect people to keep their tops on in the work-out areas because otherwise it was giving the 'wrong message'. Woman2's query to woman1 was not – as I had anticipated – how to avoid doing this awful task because it was – well – awful and the opposite of the point of a gym. No, no, no – her query was whether it was her place to do it or whether the receptionist or someone else should be making it clear to the – presumably –non-toned, non-gorgeous people that no one wanted to look at their non-perfect bodies and until they were slim and beautiful and perfect, what the hell were they doing at a gym etc. I was fascinated.

Anyhow.

Back to the scooter.

I lifted the lid and there was a large, tightly sealed, transparent plastic bag of white stuff.

I've never taken illegal drugs of any description and have rarely indulged even paracetamol or ibuprofen. I was pumped full of all kinds of wonderful chemicals during each of three births. I was happy to have anything that was going be it diamorphine or anything else. But on a day to day basis - no.

But good lord – I've seen films. I guessed immediately what it was and I further surmised that mobility scooters did not usually come with boots full of what I saw before me. Stunned, is the only word that really describes how I felt.

Not only do I have a fair idea of what a drugs stash looks like, I even know it's called a stash. And while I didn't know then that it was cocaine, I knew it was something that wasn't grass or dope or weed or whatever. I knew it was what on any cop film would be 'serious shit'. I also guessed that there must have been up to 10 lbs of it, assuming it weighs a similar amount when packed together as baking flour. I have no idea what that is in kilos even though I am pro the EU (reformed of course). But it looked like it would weigh about the same as my third baby if I were to pick it up – which I had no intention of doing. At that point I did not know there was more hidden elsewhere in the vehicle.

I just stared and stared at it in all its glaring, plastic whiteness. It was completely packed in – compressed.

My brain would not process the presence of the stuff in the small trunk with the scooter itself. Why was my groovygranz scooter stuffed with drugs? It was clearly not – if my misfiring brain was still functioning logically – someone's personal supply which could have been explained away as a very silly mistake.

Unbidden, a phrase I'd heard on the news popped into my head -'street value'. I had no idea what that might be but I was more than sure it was many times the value of the horrible scooter.

I wasn't even scared at first. I was alarmed but that is closer to shock than fear. I was certainly surprised. I was wide awake.

Then my brain started popping other words and phrases into my head like some sort of mad link-word game. There are word links they test old people's mental fitness with so that if the nurse or doctor says cat you are supposed to say dog. If they say salt you are supposed to say pepper. If they say Monday and you say Hitler then you are definitely in trouble.

Well, once my brain got hold of the concept of illegal drugs and 'street value' the words that came unbidden were, guns, violence, death, horrible death, drug lords, collateral damage (me), innocent victim (me) and more death. And that is why I nearly wet myself when another forceful knock on my front door reverberated through the flat.

Now, this next part may be harder to believe than even the arrival of drugs in the mobility scooter but I kid you not this is what went through my head, which was still sparking in all kinds of mad directions. In between stumbling up the step back into the kitchen, staggering through the kitchen and into the hallway and literally falling down the corridor towards the front door, I was in a sweat of relief thinking that van man had returned.

It's a mistake, I thought. That much was obvious. This is nothing to do with me. I do not want it to be anything to do with me. Any fantasy I may have had about myself being a good citizen just went out of the window faced with the alternative parallel world which we know is just a few yards away – just as we know we are supposedly only ever a few feet away from an urban rat. I still do not believe that. It is the most ridiculous of urban myths and only makes sense if you factor in that some folk are very close to very many rats and most of us have as much chance of meeting a rat as we do of receiving a scooter we didn't want filled with illegal drugs.

My mental babble bubbled over. The mistake will be easily dealt with when the deliver guy checks his delivery sheet or some clever app pops up on the diseased screen that everyone manhandles having never ever thought to wash their hands. He may or may not know what is in the trunk but if he does I will pretend I don't and then I will successfully race him to the lean-to/garage/not-a-greenhouse while he goes around the outside. I will, of course, first close the trunk of the scooter. I will be calm, I thought, and play up the dotty older woman routine. It can work a charm. I recall once having a burley policeman (burley is overweight when applied to a police officer) call to my house after a minor road incident. On seeing that I was a. a woman b. not white but living in a large house c. surrounded by children – he spoke to me like I was two brain cells smarter than an amoeba and advised that I wait for my husband to come home because my husband (he said all this slowly) would help me fill in all the forms. He didn't quite go as far as patting me on the head so I didn't go as far as to explain to him that I was a qualified – albeit it non-practising - lawyer and if he wanted to speak to the brains of the operation – even on a really bad day - that was definitely me. I didn't clarify because I didn't care enough and I could see that the chances of getting the stupid lump out of my house quickly so I could finish making the tea were much improved if I let him leave with his stereotypes intact.

I reached for the latch with far more enthusiasm than I had on the first occasion and maybe the idea that it might be someone else was struggling to get through and that was why I fumbled. Subconscious self-preservation. Or maybe my hands were sweaty or nerves put me off and my hand-eye co-ordination – which was never great and meant I'd never have been a tennis player even if I'd enjoyed sport – let me down. But I was determined and grabbed again and turned and pulled.

The door came in surprisingly easily maybe because it was being helped from outside. I did register in a split second that it was not van man just as the handle of something dark and very hard struck my temple and I tumbled backwards into the hallway.

I'd been struck with the butt of a gun. Just like in a gangster movie.

Chpt 5.

Premature Pete

If everything about Pete hadn't been premature I might have been dead before this story got properly started. Certainly my part in it would have been very limited. As it happens, this young man's inability to exercise basic control – even when it came to the apposite time to swing the butt of a gun into a granny's head – was a saviour.

He could have pretended to be a house caller and sussed out the situation a little before blundering in. Maybe that was the original plan. I'll never know. I do know that Pete isn't and never will be the kind of person who could reliably carry off a long-term plan.

He could have pushed me back into the hallway while I was still puzzling that he was not the guy who delivered the scooter. Plenty of time. He could have muscled in, deftly kicked the door closed behind him with his foot while either issuing a macho threat to keep me quiet or – if he was still inclined – walloping me once I was further back into the hallway – all without causing any disturbance in the neighbourhood at that time of the morning. I've seen films. That's what I'd have done. In his position. In the many scenarios I played out in the following hours, that was the one I would have chosen if I was the gangster.

But no, Mr middle height, middling appearance, goes to the gym when he can be bothered but only works his arms, part swung the gun in a semi arc losing momentum and accuracy in a fumbled impulse strike when the door was still being pulled open by me and pushed by him. Any chance of a killer or even knockout blow was dissipated. I've been hit harder by tourists on Princes St who think they are more entitled to the pavement than me although not across the temple.

The gun butt glanced off my quite robust skull, scraping the skin and causing more surprise than pain initially. It was the backwards momentum already in motion due to my pulling the door and stepping back to accommodate it plus his shove forward that actually sent me down onto my bum still not having taken enough breath to scream.

The next part is a bit of a blur but I know he actually turned away from me scrambling to shut the still open door. In my fantasy film I'd have scuttled away or – depending on the film – tried to bravely defend myself while he was distracted. Instead, I automatically went to pull down my skirt to hide my large comfy knickers and bare legs and regain some dignity. My heart was pounding and I felt fear and anger in equal measure but I was extremely clear about what was happening and why. I also knew Premature Pete was not a young man to be messed with if I didn't want him to have a second go at staving my skull in.

By the time he shut the door I'd skittered back crab like, a couple of yards, was properly upright but not standing and my skirt was back down over my legs. I stared up at him wide eyed I'm sure. He stared down at me pop-eyed and panicky. If he'd been cool and collected I think I'd have been less scared. If he'd been the cool cold type (listen to me – I talk as if this happens to me all the time - it doesn't of course) I think I would have just mentally given up and thought – oh – well – let's see how this whole getting shot to death thing pans out. The idea that I had opportunity to feed into this situation, to possibly change it and save myself felt like an overwhelming responsibility and that idea came to me because it was clear Pete had messed up and didn't really know what he was doing.

I'd already recalled in some latent still functioning part of my brain that my upstairs Polish neighbours were away in – well – Poland. Screaming was not only likely to get me shot quicker it was pointless. And that seemed a little unfair because in these flats normally you even try and fart quietly because anything louder than a gentle cough will carry on a quiet day.

If only I'd been writing Mrs Angry letters to The Guardian or the Independent. I had a good one ready about how trying to fend off a Boris Johnson premiership with sensible arguments was like trying to ward off Ebola with a flu jab. If I'd been writing I might not have answered the door in the very first place to the first man who delivered the damn scooter. Too late to think back to that now. Already there were too many loops to unpick.

"Where is it?" he yipped in a surprisingly thin voice. Scottish. Leith. Lots of English people in Edinburgh so it's worth mentioning. I have absolutely no idea where the next certainty came from but I knew – just knew – that pretending not to know what he was talking about was – at that moment – the thing most likely to get me badly injured or killed. 'Blown away' if you prefer.

"The lean-to," I said quickly and breathlessly.

"What?"

"Garage / shed / not-a-conservatory…"

Pete stared at me as if he were trying to make sense of a new species. I stared back, noticing only that the gun was still being held by the barrel. Good.

"What the FUCK are you talking about?"

Yes, I know – we may as well have been on the evening train to Newcastle. I'll edit out some of that.

"The scooter?"

Then there was a gap where everything slowed down a little and gained some much needed reality. He glanced quickly over his shoulder – checking the door presumably. Then he turned the gun around to point at me. Bad. Then he slightly relaxed his shoulders. Also bad as it suggested he thought he was back in charge of the situation – which technically he was. He straightened up demonstrating to me that he was, in fact, no taller than I am. And while I always thought of myself as tall when I was at secondary school it turns out in the modern world I'm not really that tall. All three of my daughters were taller than me by the time they were in their early teens. So – he's about 5ft 7 - some part of my brain made a note. He had dark, thinning hair, jelled in the fashion, jeans obviously, and a T-shirt that I suspected wasn't really warm enough for this morning even thought it was technically summer. But then he would have driven. No one turns up to a house with a gun looking for drugs having arrived on the bus. Do they? I was pleased to see, as I always am, that at least he wasn't wearing trainers. Trainers are not shoes.

Lord knows what kind of inventory he was making of me – if he was. Older middle-aged (these days *middle age* seems to last until you are 60 so I qualify) mixed-race woman on her own not in bad shape but far from fanciable unless you were an older man looking for a companion-cum-carer. That was probably the extent of it.

"Get up. Show me," he said with a flick of the awful gun now facing the correct way.

It was when I tried to stand that I felt a brief but strong wave of nausea and the pain in my temple. I didn't think I was going to pass out. I never have in my life even with three babies. And the pain wasn't that bad. It must have been the shock. When I consider it, I was much more bashed about the last time I got knocked down by a cyclist. And that's happened more than once.

One Friday I was walking up to the shopping centre at Chesser – on the path – on the correct side – not the side with bicycles painted on it and next thing you knew – or I knew – I was sprawled on the pavement. Being 'sprawled' on the floor at my age is never any good. Young folk can fall and fling themselves around with no ill effect but past a certain age, even a minor altercation with the ground can leave you shaken for days. Well, there I was, uncertain how I got there and unable to get up (I'm still talking about the cycling incident – stay with me). My mind was a blank. I looked to the side and saw a pair of legs, followed them up to see a tall young man in cycling gear with a startled face staring down at me asking me in a worried voice if 'anything was broken'. I said no but again found I was unable even to haul myself into a kneeling position. Maybe he thought he'd done something really bad because he just kept muttering

'Oh no oh no.' Anyhow, after a bit I managed to get to my knees then up. Oddly, one of my first sensations was embarrassment even though there didn't appear to be anyone around. And, you know, if someone is genuinely sorry and apologising it is actually quite hard to be cross with them even if you are hurt. Folk would do well to remember that when they are lying through their teeth or trying to pretend things weren't their fault when they were. So, I told him off and said he should consider that we'd be in a whole different scenario if I'd been a frail old person (I think 'old' starts at around 85 these days – God knows what you are between 60 and 85) or a child. He agreed fervently – said sorry for the umpteenth time and then was most thankful for his dismissal and rode off.

A little way down the road a woman who had come upon the scene after the guy had mown me down from behind but before I'd managed to get up did ask me if I was alright and that was nice. By the time I got to the shops however I was shaking and realised I was bleeding from my knees and elbow and hands and had a horrible pain in my shoulder and a hard swelling in my right calf where the wheel had hit me before the rest of him ploughed into the rest of me. So I went straight home.

Hey ho.

I suppose the point I'm making is that the cyclist did more damage but I forgave him because it was unintentional and he was sorry. I did not forgive Pete.

"And don't scream unless you want some more."

Being of above average intelligence I did not have to enquire as to more of what. Also, as I just mentioned, I'd already concluded that screaming would be a waste of time and risky.

Even though things were back in focus I took my time getting up. Not too much time as Pete was clearly not the patient type. Enough, I hoped, to seem less robust than I am.

"It's this way" I pointed but did not move. Instinctively I guessed it was better to let him give instructions, feel he was in charge. And no – I'm not talking about female instinct I'm talking about that preservation instinct which was fully conscious and firing on all cylinders by then. He gestured with the gun for me to move.

I turned and began to walk towards the kitchen. The hallway appeared to be warping in and out of different time space continuums, the walk seemed never ending but the hallway also seemed to have shrunk. We got to the kitchen door – I turned uncertainly. Would he want to check there was no one in there, that I was on my own? No – he'd already decided I was on my own. I suppose everything about me from the no ring to the way I was dressed, maybe even to the flat itself suggested that. I don't know. Or maybe he was just too stupid to think of it. He waved the gun at me in a way that even someone like me who knows nothing about fire arms etiquette or gun speak knew meant 'keep moving in the direction of the scooter and the drugs or you'll be sorry because I'm a man with a gun and you are a woman without one.'

We reached the lean-to/garage/not-a-conservatory, went down the single step and there it was with the boot still open. So – no chance at all that I could pretend I'd not seen the package.

"Give me your phone," he snarled.

I was not expecting that. I turned and looked at him and whether he interpreted my bemusement for insubordination or defiance or whatever, I earned myself a good hard shove backwards that would have sent me to the floor again if I'd not encountered my old silver cross pram. ['say something, say something quickly you silly cow'] that's me in my head not him. I was about to ask why he wanted to see my phone and realised in good time that was a very wrong response and so pointed, like a 3 year old who has forgotten the words for something important, back towards the kitchen. And just as I'd understood gun lingo he understood finger lingo. We were getting along like two foreign tourists from different countries stuck in a broken lift with only faded English instructions on how to escape.

Back in the kitchen I used more finger lingo to point at the table where lay my trusty blue brick shaped Nokia block button non-smart-phone. He looked at the phone, looked at me and then back at the phone.

"What the (yes he said it again) is THAT?" I'll insert the word 'fly' from now on.

He continued –

"What the flying hell is this flying piece of flying shit?"

"My phone"

"You're flying with me?"

"No."

He looked at the phone and cut a side stare at me desperately trying to weigh up if I was lying or not. It took me a few seconds but it suddenly dropped like a large unsecured bolt mechanism from badly constructed scaffolding – he wanted to check if I'd photographed the stash and sent it out into cyberspace. I hadn't. I couldn't. If he believed me I was saved again for the second time in almost as many minutes.

"Sit down and put your hands on the table and don't move."

I did as I was told, feeling, I have to say, tense and a bit weepy as you do after a shock. It was a relief to sit down even under the circumstances.

He picked up the phone and examined it as if it were a mysterious medieval relic rather than a phone that was perfectly useful for texting and making phone calls. He pressed a few buttons and presumably established that the last time it had been used was last night. Long before the delivery of the flying scooter (sorry).

"This is it?" he said, staring around as if a smart phone might jump out at him from behind the fridge. But then his gaze was distracted. Maybe he was marking other missing items; no dishwasher, no microwave. How much time would a man like him spend in the kitchen? I do not like to make assumptions about folk but it did cross my mind that unless a meal was placed in front of him he'd be the sort to pick up the phone rather than the saucepan. But whether the missing essential kitchen items registered or not something clearly fitted a pattern because I could see by the expression on his face that he had reluctantly accepted the idea that the phone was my phone and the only phone and for now at least he did not have to contend with the idea that anyone other than him, me and possibly amazon Al knew the scooter and its interesting contents were not where they were supposed to be. And that was confirmed by his next question.

"Who lives upstairs?"

Feeling the way I did and under different conditions I would have said 'my neighbours'. I can be a bit cussed that way. As it was I batted straight and said,

"Lana and Bartek and their little girl, they are away in Poland."

"We'll check," he threw back.

Two things struck me about that. Firstly, although he said he'd check he clearly believed me secondly he said 'we'. I didn't like that bit.

The next few minutes were a pantomime of him ordering me to do things in my own home and me doing them. Immediately.

The trunk of the scooter was closed by me under Pete's instructions. I do not see why because it's not as if the drugs were going anywhere and anyone breaking into the lean-to/thingy wasn't going to ignore the presence of a brand new scooter. Anyhow the door was also locked but the door entering into the lean-to thingy from my kitchen was propped open with a broom handle by me, again under Pete's direction.

We then had a brief tour around my flat – presumably so Pete could get the lay of the land. The thing that began to dawn on me while we did this was that he didn't have any intention of leaving any time soon. I didn't like that either as you can imagine. At some point I requested the loo. Now I know what you are thinking. In the movies everyone seems to be able to hold their bladders forever. Well that is nonsense. And frankly – if you are stressed – the thing your bladder wants to do most of all is let go of its contents. There was surprisingly little objection to that although Pete had first to check that I couldn't escape out of the bathroom window – I couldn't easily do that – and then insisted on the door being left ajar. Well, I've had three babies as I've told you at least twice now and weeing within hearing of other human beings doesn't hold any shame for me. Good lord, after my second I had to wee with two nurses in the toilet cubicle with me in case I keeled over. They'd established that I was dangerously anaemic. I was also, at the time, very large and there was no way just one of them would have been able to prevent me going head first off the loo.

So I peed. It was a relief I can tell you.

We checked the bedroom. Double bed but no evidence of a man. He may have not been deliberately looking for that but the more he looked around the more ridiculous macho swagger he seemed to adopt – or regain. How would I know? I'd never seen him before.

Then we got to the living room. He had a good look. Pictures of my daughters and my gorgeous grandchildren. I didn't want him looking at those. That was the first time I felt anger rising over everything else. I supressed it. A mirror. The living room is self-decorated with – I have to admit – a colour I call 'everything that was left in the shed mixed together and white added.' You'd probably call it dusky pink and that is thanks to the tiny amount of dark red from when my youngest daughter briefly had her bedroom wall painted red. At least it wasn't black.

Then we came back out into the hall. Then we went back into the living room. Then out into the hall. Then back into the living room. Then he stood in the middle of the room waving the gun around in more of a lazy gesture than a threatening one but one which was still alarming if you happened to be standing in the general direction of where the gun was occasionally pointing.

"Where is it?"

"Where is what?"

Then I got it. He may not have consciously registered the missing regarded-as-essential items in the kitchen but he did in the living room. And we said it together -

"The TV" only I said it as a statement and he said it as a question.

"Don't have one." I said flatly.

And he said – "Oh – you're one of *those*."

Cheeky git.

And that is when the door was knocked loudly for the third time that morning only this time the knocking felt unnervingly as if it were coming from inside my skull.

Chpt 6.

Frankie needs a pee

When my door was assaulted for a third time, I couldn't help breaking out into the proverbial cold sweat. The previous two visitations had led to nothing good and I'm a fast learner. Suddenly I understood how those gentlewomen felt who got 'the vapours' in Victorian or faux Victorian novels. I could sense my heartrate accelerate and my skin become clammy and I became a little woozy again. At my age it could also have been a hot flush but I had the menopause early thankfully.

Pete tensed then darted out into the hallway gripping the gun more firmly. Then he leaned back into the living room where I'd managed to remain standing. He pointed the gun at me. Why me? I wasn't the one knocking at the door. Then he gestured with his free left hand for me to move towards him. I pointed at him with a questioning face – he nodded. We were like some poor quality mime act at the Fringe. He backed into the hall still gesturing. I moved forward desperately reading his face for clues as to where this was going and trying but failing to not look at the gun. Then he backed down the hall making way for me to move past him towards the front door. No more gestures needed; I'm quite quick on the uptake as I've already mentioned. I was to answer the door with him standing behind me.

What if it was the police, I hear you ask. (Well – I surmise you might be asking that at this point. I would.) Who would have called them? Would the police come that quickly unless they knew there was a gun and it was likely to be a bit more exhilarating than someone with suspiciously missing garden ornaments? And if they did know there was a gun would they really stroll up and knock on the door? No. I didn't get the impression Pete was bright but even he will have guessed it would be junk mail, charity sellers or people who think they are entitled to take up your time doing surveys about cleaning products you don't use or social policies that are never going to be implemented. I did once spend nearly ten minutes answering a survey where you were promised a free box of chocolates. We all have levels of self-interest that may surprise even ourselves.

I glanced over my shoulder nervously to see Pete almost entirely disappeared in the kitchen with just the tip of the gun and enough of his head to let one eye view. I flicked my hands in a little 'what now?' gesture and he dipped the quickest of nods to indicate that I should proceed to the door without making a fuss, take a deep breath and open said door and do whatever was required to get rid of the posty or the surveyor or the chugger or whomever, or something unpleasant would happen and I didn't really need to know what and couldn't think anyway because it had already been a very trying morning.

But just as I reached one hand out to the door handle and one to the latch – you have to do both to open the door – and – I thought - if I ever get out of this I am definitely getting a security chain, there was a shrill yell.

"Pete! Pete... Frankie needs to pee," in an Italian accent and a female voice.

Then things sped up remarkably. There was another rap on the door and I heard a child's voice "Peeeeete" and the man in question stomped up the hall behind me yanked the partially open door right back while shoving me for the second time in my own hallway so that I was, this time, squashed against the wall partly by the door and partly by him. He then dragged the person who had been on my step into the hall and slammed the door.

The person he hauled into my hallway was a plump pretty woman, shorter than me but with a big presence whose name, it turned out, was Carla. Carla was, indeed, Italian although she had bleached blonde hair and bad roots. She had a large shoulder bag over – well – her shoulder and was carrying a little boy on her ample curvaceous hips, who was more than capable of walking and far too big to be carried.

All four of us stayed cramped in the tiny hallway with me wedged against the wall, Carla and the little boy I presume was the Frankie in question, on the other side of Pete while he leaned his gun hand against the door and gesticulated with his free hand – his mime hand. Though, at this point, he didn't use hand signals with Carla.

"WHAT THE FLY ARE YOU DOING YOU STUPID COW I TOLD YOU TO STAY IN THE FLYING CAR WHILE I CHECKED OUT THE OLD BAG"

That wasn't very nice – but then Carla added a few new words to the expletive lexicon that would put hairs on your chest. In the interests of literature we'll amalgamate them all into the one replacement.

"DON'T SPEAK TO ME LIKE THAT YOU FLYING FLY. YOU SAID YOU WERE GOING TO BE IN AND OUT IN TWO MINUTES JUST LIKE WHEN WE'RE FLYING

YOU FLYING PIG. FRANKIE NEEDS A PEE AND SO DO I AND WE WERE SUPPOSED TO BE GETTING SOMETHING TO EAT. WHY DO WE HAVE TO SIT IN THE FLYING CAR STARVING AND NEEDING A PEE BECAUSE AL MESSED THINGS UP AGAIN AFTER YOU SAID YOU WOULDN'T USE HIM NO MORE…" All in a sexy Italian accent but she never said 'ciao baby' which I always say to my brother's Italian partner. She doesn't seem to mind even after a couple of decades…

Carla was even shorter than I'd thought at first. I was able to get a good look at her while they had their little family exchange. Average sized Pete stood over her by a couple of inches even though she was wearing shoes I couldn't have walked in when I was 20. Her plump but tiny feet were practically perpendicular to the floor. She wore lots of perfectly applied make up including very red lipstick – headache inducing red at that time of the morning - on pouty full lips and would have been very pretty if she hadn't been so hard faced.

The little cutie on her womanly hip was snuggled into her exposed and impressive bosom. He looked really comfortable. She didn't really look Italian on closer inspection. But there you go. Even I am at the mercy of stereotypes.

In a 1950s movie this little Trixie would have been poured into some tight fitting satin with every dip, curve and hollow on display including the acres of fleshy bosom, hair bleached more professionally and piled high, with men tripping over themselves to get the chance to burry parts of their body into all that sweet mallow. Nowadays, I suspect she was strapped in with spandex and permanently wishing she looked like a scarecrow. Like Pete, she exuded tension – which is a polite way of saying she also swore a lot. Not good for me.

Frankie was a whole different kettle of fish. As mum and dad (?) continued their 'conversation' his big chocolate button eyes settled on me still squashed in the corner not daring to upset the delicate balance of family dynamics. But he suddenly blew my cover by smiling, pointing at me and chirruping,

"Who's she?" in a sweet, soft, curious, child's voice.

They both stopped as if noticing me for the first time. Pete stepped back so that it was women and children – child – at the door end of the hall and then him a bit further up looking at us. Me, the unwanted guest in My Own Home.

Carla looked from me to him, gestured at the child while thrusting, huffing and speaking volumes with her whole body (maybe they are a pantomime mime family) and simply saying "PEEEEE". So, yes, also taking more than her fair share of vowels.

Then things kind of got moving again like after you've stopped a DVD for a tea break and you've had a stretch and are back on the sofa ready for the rest of the film. Yes I do have a DVD player.

Pete spoke to Carla

"The toilet is down there but you need to go check on any neighbours."

She was clearly not in the best of moods and didn't want to be ordered about.

"Youuuu go check your flying self" albeit now in a strange stage whisper having, presumably, remembered why they were there.

Frankie started jigging up and down on Carla's hip repeating,

"Pee, pee, pee"

And yours truly stepped forward bold as you like and said,

"I'll take him." I put out my arms and Frankie just leaned into them.

And before you know it I'm in the loo with lovely Frankie – with the door open obviously – the Italian bit is off to the upstairs neighbour and the other neighbour close enough to have heard, with some cock and bull story about a wrong address no doubt at the ready and Pete is pacing from the loo door back to the front door waiting for peachy Carla to return.

Frankie starts, like any child would, on the who-are-you, what's-your-name, do-you-live-here never ending child's verbal conveyor belt. And I ask him a few questions and learn that he is Frankie, he is 'nearly four', he likes cars, his friend is called Tiemba. Tiemba is lucky because, Frankie tells me, he has two mummies. I love conversations like this. It reminds me that if we don't obliterate the planet – these children could grow up thinking racism and bigotry is as all just a mad part of the past. They will just grow up with children of other races and cultures sitting right next to them at school – in places like this I mean. Not like the last place I lived.

We are brutally interrupted by Pete who tells Frankie in no uncertain terms to "shut up". I am upset but then surprised when I look into Frankie's big soft brown eyes with an escaped brown curl hanging over his heart-shaped olive face, to see that although he complies immediately he is not scared. It's like he obeys for a quiet life. I am glad. Carla must be some cookie. He knows, for now, he is safe. Miniature peachy mummy has his back and so she bloody well should if she is going to carry on with the likes of Pete. *Carry on Carla* like a bad 1960s comedy starring Sid James. That almost makes me laugh – but it won't quite come. Contemplating being brutally killed in your own home can cause a bit of comedic constipation.

My next thought is along the same line – well it would be wouldn't it. In my position would you be able to think of anything else? At some point during Pete's pacing he has come to the conclusion I came to while Carla was trashing his manhood. He will have to shoot me.

One very ordinary looking man whose name I didn't even know and whose appearance was, you will not be surprised to learn, of secondary interest to me after 'where is the gun pointing' might have walked away from this debacle with a few threats about not calling the police – they won't believe you anyway – there will be consequences etc. etc. etc. but who is not going to remember a tiny sexy Italian bleached blonde and an adorable boy with curly brown hair and a Scottish/Italian accent?

He is going to have to kill me now.

More than that he wants to and having to is just a tantalizing side dish.

I began to feel very unwell. Almost like seasickness.

It was like when I arrived at the shops after getting flattened by the bike. I had thought I was ok but I was wrong. I have lovely daughters and sons-in-law and beautiful grandchildren – better than anyone else's obviously – and I want to go and visit them and take them all sorts of things they probably don't want and will bin when I'm gone. I could've started crying then but I didn't. Wrong generation for all that blubbing.

I took a deep breath and looked at Frankie.

"Would you like a drink?"

"Milkshake and a cookie" he says without hesitation, smiling and doing up his trousers.

He is nearly four and I am a grown up woman so it doesn't occur to him that I won't have what he wants and as it happens I have. I could easily make a fresh milkshake with milk and fruit in a blender but I also have some of that horrible powdered stuff because my youngest daughter brought it home from university last time she was here. That will have to do for now – all culinary creativity has flown from me. I'm not sure I could switch the whizzer on. Maybe I wouldn't need to as my hands are shaking. I could just put everything in a beaker and hold it for a minute. Me = human blender.

Frankie takes my hand.

I feel a little calmer.

We pootle into the kitchen. Out of the corner of my eye (everything seems more than focused now, very stark and clear with sharp edges. It is as if someone fixed my eyesight and I can see the way I did when I was young without the need for specs) and see Pete watching us. And because the mental clarity is like the visual clarity I can almost hear his thoughts. He is trying to think if there is any reason he shouldn't let me and Frankie go into the kitchen. Maybe he remembers we locked the lean-to/garage thingy. And anyhow – it's so full of stuff I couldn't get out faster than any bullet he might send in my direction. Would he shoot me in front of Frankie? What a ridiculous question. How would someone who would never take drugs and never use a firearm answer that question about a man like Pete.

Ignoring all else, I tell Frankie to sit at the table. While he climbs up onto the chair quite willingly and interested in everything around him, I fetch milk from the fridge and the powder from the cupboard. And because little children love to do all the things we have begun to think of as mundane I let him scoop out a heaped spoon of brown powder (it is chocolate milkshake powder) and then I let him pour in the milk. The carton is not too heavy as there isn't much milk left inside. Then I give him a small whisk, not much longer than a table spoon and he grins delightedly looking from me to the implement in his hand. And because I have caught the mime contagion from Pete, instead of saying –'you use it to stir in the powder and make the milk a bit frothy' I just make a whisking motion with my hand and he gets it.

While he is whisking and examining his progress and then whisking again, I go down a more calming thought alley. I realise I can hear no conversations either to the side or overhead so unless Carla is incredibly slow there is no one home. Good for them. Bad for me. Or maybe not. If there is no one around would Pete think it worth the risk to just leave me tied up? Doubt it.

I turn my attention back to Frankie. I wonder if he is too old for a buggy. I have a good one. It was one I got from a skip but, instead of selling this one I kept it. It's one of the 3-wheel types with pneumatic tyres and quite a good one. I looked it up online and they cost about £400 quid new for a basic model. One of the rear wheels was flat but just needed pumping up with my old bicycle pump. The front one was flat but that needed a puncture repair kit. I presume it ended up in the skip because some lazy man or woman couldn't be bothered to fix the inner tube. £400 in the skip. I decided to keep this one for my grandson. He is a bit younger than Frankie and getting too old for a buggy but I am getting too old to haul him about and this one can go over rough terrain when we walk along the river and if he gets tired he can hop in for a bit without doing my back in.

I started bringing buggies home last summer. Initially it was the waste that was bugging me (excuse the pun). You'd see them in the early morning out on the pavement by the bins. Often they were filthy dirty but otherwise in good condition. I felt a bit conspicuous bringing the first one home. Well, you can imagine what it looked like, me pushing a dirty empty buggy. Maybe folk thought I was one of those bag women or one of those lunatics that put dogs in prams. Anyway – I got the blessed thing home without much idea what I was going to do with it but sure I could not walk passed one more buggy that was going to end up in landfill. I washed it with some washing up liquid, sluiced it down with clean, warm water and left it to dry in the garden. When it was dry I photographed it and put it on Gumtree for £12. A young woman bought it. She was going on holiday the very next day and didn't want her very expensive buggy at the mercy of the baggage handlers, sensible woman. She was delighted. I was very pleased.

Since then there were dozens. The cheapest one I sold for £5, I actually found it shoved under a hedge. The most expensive one I sold for £70. It was one of those huge things with fantastic suspension. They cost over a grand new and this one – like the others - needed cleaning but all the soft coverings were removable so it was just a case of shoving them in the washing machine. Some idiot person had tried to fold it with the closing mechanism in the wrong place so it looked wonky but I sorted that. I am very handy. Even though it was a beautiful pram and a massive bargain it took the longest to sell. My eldest daughter pointed out to me that with those sorts of prams parents actually want to fork out the money. That is part of the point. It's not just about having a top-of-the-range pram it's about telling folk how much you paid for it. Well that was a strange one for me. As someone who loves nothing more than informing people that my top or skirt or the trousers they just admired cost £3 at my favourite charity shop, it's just another example of how not part of everything I am.

Just then I was ejected from my very pleasant escapism by yet another knock on my poor ill-treated front door. At least for the first time in what was a very strange day, I had a fair idea who it would be.

Pete stuck his unwelcome head into the kitchen and growled,

"Behave. I don't want to have to hurt you."

Liar, I thought and looked down at Frankie just in time to see him gulping the last of the chocolate flavoured milk.

"Cookie?" he said and smiled up at me showing chocolate stained teeth to go with his gorgeous chocolate button eyes.

Chpt 7.

Delicious, healthy, home-made, gluten-free, veggie sausages

Carla and Pete were having another not particularly muted exchange in the hall by which I surmised they were both satisfied that I was alone not just in the flat but in the building. Every few moments one or the other of them would briefly appear in the doorway and scan the kitchen to make sure I hadn't squeezed through the window over the sink, set up smoke signals or was tapping Morse code on the plumbing pipes. Actually it would be a little difficult to do the latter because they are those plastic flexi pipes now that come loose and play havoc with your boiler pressure, not copper.

What neither of them seemed to worry about was that a complete stranger might harm their child. They just left Frankie with me. They didn't ask for my police clearance certificate or anything. They had no way of knowing that, as an ex-Sunday school teacher I did actually have one.

Parents.

Then something very unsettling happened. They both went quiet and just stepped into the kitchen and stared first at me then at Frankie. He (Pete) just stared. She stared at me but smiled at the boy who smiled back with crumbs and chocolate all around his little gob. They both had their smart phones in their hands. I'm fairly sure the shape of the human hand will soon modify into that of a smart phone. He, thankfully, had put the gun somewhere. Jacket pocket? Trouser pocket? Back of his belt like in the movies? I didn't care. Away and not pointing at me were two steps in the extremely right direction.

But when I tried to catch her eye Carla looked away. Not so good.

She was sulky if you want one word to sum her up.

"Frankie, go watch the TV in the living room. We need to talk to this lady." She pronounced living room 'leeveeng rrroom'

"Annie." I said quickly. Seizing what seemed like a chance. "He can call me Granny Annie"

"He doesn't need to know your name" she spat back.

Hmmm. Really not good. And she looked at me as if I'd just trodden on her tiny toes and not apologised rather than as if she had invaded my home without a by your leave. I tried to stare her out but she did that thing where the hands are momentarily flexed, the hip goes to one side and a 'yes - and?' expression takes over the facial features. All three of my own daughters could do it in their teens. This piece wasn't anywhere near as good as my eldest daughter and she was much older than when my first child perfected it at about the age of 15. But I pretended to be chastened. Little madam.

Then he interrupted. Pete not Frankie.

"She hasn't got one."

"One what?" (Carla)

"She hasn't got a flying TV." Pete snapped as if Carla was a moron and he had not been flummoxed by the same absence.

And both Carla and Frankie stared at me as if I've just grown a third ear in the middle of my forehead and said in unison,

"What do you do?"

That is always the question. Not 'what do you do instead of watching telly?' just 'What do you do?' as if I found a way to live without oxygen.

I could have gone through the whole history of how I gave up on the box-for-the-brain-dead last century. How I've not missed it. How moronic I find it whenever I am in someone's house who is incapable of turning the damn thing off even when they have visitors. But I didn't. I realised long ago that in just the half century or so that it's been a staple in almost every home, it rules. TV Rules OK.

Younger folk don't actually find the absence quite so odd because they spend more of their time online anyway.

I could explain it's hard enough to find time to do what I want to do in a day even without what my mother still loves to call a 'proper job'. If I had to watch people compete for points on a board answering questions about celebrities I'd never heard of or has-been attention seekers eating crawling things in a for-TV jungle setting, the bread wouldn't get buttered. But I decided it was best not to go into those things.

"I do have a DVD player and lots of children's films. Should I put one of those on for Frankie?"

Carla tensed and Pete actually shuffled his feet when I said the child's name. Somewhere down inside I notch this up on the positive side of the list of reasons why I may or may not be alive at the end of the day.

And suddenly we were just like a normal, modern, dysfunctional family. Mum and possibly dad were in the kitchen at my table talking in lowered but unfriendly voices – about me I presume but maybe not. They must have a lot on their minds. I was in the living room with Frankie pretending everything is ok.

Pete took the precaution of locking the door with the turn key and appropriating it so there was no way I could make a dash for freedom.

Frankie and I watched *The Iron Giant* – which he had not seen before and loved. I chose it because it's fairly easy for an adult to watch. It's an animation but it's not sugary and stupid. And you probably won't believe this, I hardly believe it myself but part way through I briefly nodded off.

From what I recall of where we were in the film when I lost concentration and the fact that we were a good way through when Carla kicked my foot to check if I was dead, I must have drifted for over 10 minutes. However tired I am I never nap during the day. It just shows what shock and a gun butt to the forehead, however ineptly aimed, can do.

"I thought you were dead," she said and though I was blurry I could have sworn she sounded disappointed. Maybe she understood enough about the law to know that if I died unintentionally from the bump to the bonce it would be a whole different matter to the UK criminal justice system than if

I died having been shot in cold blood. I suspected neither of them were strangers to the back of a police van or the inside of a court room. When I said I was sorry to disappoint here she just sniffed. That episode went in the things- not-looking-rosy column.

Again it was Frankie who managed to deflate the taut atmosphere.

"I'm huuuuungry".

I do think children have a formal extra vowel allowance up until about the age of 7.

He looked at Carla; Carla scowled at Pete who had followed her in. Pete positively glowered at me lifting his lip briefly in what could only be described as a dog-like snarl face. What a family. I, on the other hand, used words.

"I'd be more than happy to get you all something to eat. It must be lunch time."

In fact it wasn't lunchtime which for me is 1pm. Still, a great deal of the morning had passed. How time flies etc.

Pete was still glowering and looking as if he were trying to think of a reason why I shouldn't make them a meal of which there were quite a few that I could think of. He, on the other hand seemed unable to come up with one so he just shrugged.

"What do you have?" demanded Carla. She looked as if she enjoyed her food. Good. And because it's what I would always do under... well, I was going to say 'under the circumstances' but as you probably guessed I'd never been under any circumstances remotely like these so I should say – what I would do faced with a hungry group I'd not planned for and if there wasn't either a pot of soup on the hob or vegetable curry. Situations covered by this would include; Daughter no. 3 arriving home with uni friends, Daughter no.1 arriving with family having told me they would have eaten only for them to arrive actually all hungry. Daughter no.2 suddenly deciding when everyone else is fed and the plates wiped clean that actually she is not as full as she thought she was and could she have something even though she'd said she didn't want anything. Delicious, healthy, home-made, gluten-free veggie sausages, which I make in batches and keep in the freezer.

Carla surprised me saying, "Good. Is healthy". Frankie, maybe just registering the word sausage piped up, "With chips?" to which I was able to reply, thanks to the fact that I have not rejected the use of a fridge with a reasonable freezer compartment in my attitude to technology – "Yes if you would like". He would definitely like. And sauce. Pete rolled his eyes, wiggled his thumb at me – to indicate I should go to the kitchen (I was fairly sure he wasn't hitchhiking) then he followed me into the kitchen and closed the door meaningfully which I did not like at all. I took a shuddery breath.

The door adjoining the lean-to was still ajar and I got a glimpse of the blessed scooter like a malignant, over-sized ladybug just sitting there. Yes – this is all your fault, I thought. Realising that Pete wasn't the kind of man to follow a woman into a kitchen to ask if he should lay the table, I turned carefully to face him with my back against the sink.

"Let's get a few things straight here. I've got serious business to attend to and I don't want things fly'd up by a stupid old black bitch." He sneered.

So, that's how it was going to be, I thought. He's going to get himself fired up with a bit of good old racism and misogyny in case the dirty deed had to be done, which he seemed to have concluded it probably did sooner or later. He went on.

"We're all going to stay calm, not get in each other's way. You (he jabbed his finger at me, perhaps in case I'd forgotten who I was) are going to do as you're told if you know what's good for you and you seem to. (Was he trying to butter me up while making it clear he might have to kill me?) These are the rules. You don't answer the door unless I tell you. Keep away from the windows as far as possible. (I presume he was going through some regular gangster fantasy because there was a 7 ft. hedge in front of the house and just our garden to the rear.) Don't talk to the kid unless absolutely necessary, do as you're told as quietly as possible and we all might come out of this ok. I've got problems here and I don't want you to add to them because then I'd have to make you disappear and I don't want to do that. (Oh yes you do) Capice?" (Dear lord – he thinks he's Marlon Brando.)

Up close (and he was, by then, standing right in front of me – I unconsciously stooped a little to make myself smaller – it's a thing women do) you can see that he has quite bad skin and spends too much time on the tanning bed and probably dyes his hair although he can't be more than 33. Under the orange veneer he is sallow and his breath smells as if he has a nervous stomach.

Then he straightens up and steps back as if concluding the little chat before adding one thing. "Someone else will be coming this afternoon to help keep things straight here. We are going to be staying with you as your guests (he half smirks when he says this last word) until this flying mess can all be sorted out tomorrow morning then – well - we'll be gone" (and so will I. My mind adds this without any invitation from me).

For some bizarre reason I never fathomed, my mouth ran away with itself – which is not a habit of mine.

"Who else is coming?"

To which Pete, not surprisingly, lost his rag as they say.

"This is exactly what I am talking about. NONE OF YOUR BUSINESS. You flying nosey old cow. You do not need to know. Someone else is coming to help me get out of this shitting, flying situation that should never have happened in the first place and wouldn't have happened if you hadn't got the wrong flying mobility scooter. You don't even need one you lazy flying bitch."

Then the door to the kitchen burst open.

"Is big Bruce coming, is he? Is he? Is Uncle Bruce coming here? Is he going to come on holiday with us when we leave Granny Annie's?" said Frankie with a huge beaming smile.

"Shut the fly uuuuuuup!" That was Pete and he was also making free with extra vowels. But Carla stepped in, hips waggling, arms akimbo, carefully plucked eyebrows very raised.

"No baby." (And it did not sound like a term of endearment) "Don't speak to Frankie like that I told you. Don't do it."

This time Frankie was shaken and backed into Carla's legs with his little mouth turned down but to my extreme surprise Pete took a huge breath and got himself under control. And although he didn't sound any less like a mean motherflyer, he lowered the volume.

"Ok. Okaaaay"

And I had to hand it to Carla. Whatever was going on here, as far as her child was concerned, she had some instincts. Mama bear wasn't letting baby bear get mauled by the mangy, flea-bitten hyena any time soon even if she chose to bed down with it. And looking out for baby bear is always a mamma bear's job.

"But now she knows even more…" said Pete in a very unpleasant, false, sing-song voice.

He may as well have added – 'so we'll HAVE to shoot her and it's all your fault.'

But I pretended that all of this was Greek to me. Not just to them but I think I tried to pretend to myself too that I couldn't see where this was going. It was just too unpleasant.

"Right, I'll get the food on." I concluded in my most matter-of-fact way.

As I sorted the food, I occasionally peered out of the small kitchen window to the screened sidewalk. Along to the left was the back garden. It seemed a long way off. I felt I'd not been out there for a year although it was just yesterday. I'd had a wash out and then had to dash and get it an hour later because it started to spot. In the end it was just one of those showers where you are better leaving the washing out but I didn't know that. I put it back out. There has been a lot of torrential rain recently cut by periods of suffocating heat that has no place in Scotland. So there is usually a clothes horse, draped with almost dry clothes in the back bedroom with the small bed and the cot and all the grandkids' paraphernalia. I tried to remember what I'd done the day before apart from rescuing and re-hanging washing and I could not recall one single thing.

Some time later my new unwanted family were sat at my table eating my home-made veggie sausages with oven chips and frozen peas with all the usual condiments that go on food like that. Carla had a glass of water. Frankie had some more milk – of which we were running short and Pete had a cup of tea – weak, two sugars. I had a cup of tea, strong, milk, no sugar and a large slice of bread with butter. I couldn't face the cooked food but didn't want to keel over and make myself more vulnerable to being treated like yesterday's rubbish.

Initially, Frankie picked and poked at the strange looking sausages. Carla encouraged him by enthusiastically eating hers and smiling and making yummy noises and eventually he was tucking in. Honestly, Pete may have been an irredeemable pig but if it weren't for the dreadful hair, too much make-up, willingness to get involved with dangerous men and drugs and violence, she wasn't that bad.

Pete curled his lip at the food but I noticed that, after smothering everything in ketchup he at the lot. I offered them some of yesterday's lemon cake. Carla refused as if I'd offered her cyanide but then she got out one of those silly vaping machines that smell like plug-in air fresheners (and if they don't wreck your lungs in a whole new way I'm a monkey's uncle) while Pete got out a traditional cancer stick and – maybe out of habit – went over into the lean-to with the scooter and smoked there. But Frankie had a large piece of cake, scoffed it all and licked his fingers. Then Pete gestured Frankie to follow him out of the kitchen. Carla gave him one of her 'be careful with my baby or I rip your jugular out' looks and we women were left alone for a while.

I set about clearing plates and preparing to wash up. Carla didn't strike me as the washing up sort – not with those nails.

Once the sink was full and I was working away, I glanced at her and judged it was safe to ignite a conversation, which I did tentatively. I had to 'make human' with someone or my goose was well and truly cooked. As Frankie didn't have any direct influence or power in this scenario, the fact that he seemed to like me counted for very little.

As it happened, I didn't have to try and start up a conversation because Carla kicked one off by asking me how I'd made the sausages. I told her the ingredients briefly trying not to sound too much as if I were attempting to ingratiate myself, which I was.

"But how you get that great texture?"

"Ah. That really is the clever part. I saw it on a YouTube video done by a young Indian woman. Once you've got the things shaped, you pop them in a steamer for 10 minutes. Then you can handle them easily and you get that nice sausage texture. And you can chill them and freeze them."

"You're kidding me? That's real good. I will make for my Frankie. I like him to eat healthy."

She seemed genuinely pleased so I risked segueing to another other topic.

"Why does this Bruce need to come? Isn't it another – well - complication?" I asked as delicately as I could. I did not like the sound of 'Big' Bruce.

"We have busy day tomorrow. To clear this all up. (She gestured around my kitchen with her free hand as if my neat kitchen was the problem) and Frankie needs to sleep. We need someone to watch you tonight while me and Pete are in your room. I am ovulating and we are trying to get a baby. It's not working. So we have the scooter problem but we need to – how do you say - multi task."

Well, that's one way of putting it I thought.

"Big Bruce will secure you (!). Pete and I will have your bed. You can put Frankie to bed. He likes you" Here she suddenly, briefly smiles at me. It is a genuine smile of a woman who thinks anyone in the world is blessed if her son favours them. "When Frankie is asleep, Bruce will watch you so that Pete can do me." For a second I thought she had miss-spoken. Maybe she meant to say 'so Pete can 'help' me. Then I realised that she did me 'do'. She wanted Pete to 'do' her while she was ovulating so she could get her new baby. Well that is not the way to get pregnant I could have told her. These days you have to maximise the chance of sperm meeting egg in multiple ways. Knowing when you are technically ovulating won't make up for all the Western men who were left in nappies well past the age of 12 months because of lazy parenting and disposable nappies and can't make enough sperm. And later on I did get the chance to tell her but not then.

A little while after all that when, thanks to the bread and butter and the tea I felt a bit better, the blessed front door went again. And even though I was quite stressed and very tired and am not Sherlock Holmes it didn't need a genius to work out that it was probably Big Bruce.

Chpt 8.

Big Bruce

Again, I was the one sent to open the door. This time, both Premature Pete and Peachy Carla (it would have been better if she'd been called Penny) – Carnal Carla (?) watched from the kitchen. Maybe Frankie watched too. I don't know. I don't have eyes in the back of my head despite what I used to tell my children.

And if it wasn't Big Bruce but some surprise saviour – what were they going to do – all jump me, drag me back into the house screaming that I was a mad aunt with psychopathic tendencies who needed to be kept from public view and shoo whoever it was away? But knowing the modern world, maybe BB texted them (or sent some sort of electronic message) along the lines of 'walking up the path' 'knocking on the door now' so nothing was left to chance. Apart from yours truly, who is always out of any loop.

Frankie had discovered that the small second bedroom was where I kept the things my grandson liked to play with and I could hear happy playing noises. In other words, a small child talking to himself, occasionally making animal and engine noises and shuffling items of interest around. Then I heard train sounds so he must have found the little wooden primary-coloured train that used to belong to my middle daughter and which is a favourite of all the children who find it.

So, there I was answering my door yet again, not for my own guests / post / unwanted visitor but, like some tame house slave in *Gone with the Wind,* answering the door to a bloke invited by a busty, bleach-blonde, Italian Scarlet O'Hara and Rhett Butler if he'd been shorter, less charismatic and from Leith.

Bruce was big. He filled the door frame. Maybe I was a little bit off my head by this point (who needs drugs when fear will have the same effect) but for a moment I wondered how he'd ever get into my tiny flat.

As soon as they had confirmed it was who they wanted it to be, Pete dashed forwards and yanked me back although this time I managed to avoid ending up on the floor with my skirt up around my knickers or being squashed behind the door. Quite an achievement. Without even waiting for hand signals, I scuttled back into the kitchen where Carla and Frankie and I were soon joined by Pete and Big Bruce.

Even in the little time I'd had since I first heard his name, to imagine his physical appearance – and you can bet I did, I had created an entirely different person in my head. You have to remember I was overstretched in the Coping and Remaining Calm department. This was not a normal weekday for me. And, once you hear a name like that of course it kicks things off in your head. It was all getting very 'gangsta' and not at all 'Edinbra'.

First I imagined someone like that guy with the metal teeth in the old James Bond film back in the Sean Connery days when JB was still suave and sophisticated or sexist and a crass, depending on your mood. Then – whiplashing forward somewhat in the wild rollercoaster ride that was my mind – I imagined Dwayne 'The Rock' Johnson. Wrong again. Big Bruce was more Big 'The Pudding' Bruce. Yes he was about 6ft 3 and yes he was almost as wide as the door but you would have been hard pressed to find the muscles supporting that frame. He had a mop of dark, badly cut hair (maybe no one could reach it), oily skin and hands like the coal shed shovels. He could have been anywhere from 25 to 35 in age and there was no way those muscles were going to hold everything in vaguely human form much longer. It looked like the fat was already winning. He wore a black T-shirt under an old too-tight leather jacket and sweat pants that had seen a lot of sweat but never ever a running track or football field. He smelled primarily of enclosed spaces, washing left on radiators for days and fried food. Plus, his body odour was enough to make your eyeballs dissolve.

Whether by my lead I do not know but we all ended up back in my modest kitchen. Carla, Pete and I took up one side of the table and Big Bruce took up every other particle of space. The men interacted with actual words while Carla slouched with her arms folded and I stood like a spare pudding.

"Did you speak to Fixer Fred?" (Pete)

"Aye" (Bruce)

"We good to go tomorrow?" (Pete)

"Aye" (Bruce)

"The other car tanked up?" (Pete)

"Yeah" (Bruce)

"Onward travel?" (Pete)

"Aye" (Bruce)

"Documents? Somewhere to stay?" (Pete)

"Aye, aye." (Bruce)

"The Receiver cool to wait until tomorrow?" (Pete)

"Did you get Frankie's teddy?" (Carla)

"Aye. Aye." (Bruce)

Being an old Star Trek fan, I wouldn't have been surprised if he'd added 'Captain'

Her priorities sorted, Carla exited the kitchen – presumably in search of Frankie.

Ok – you get the idea. I know the two men are starting to sound like a poor quality travel agent and a not very discerning customer booking a very cheap last minute holiday to an undesirable destination but what I gleaned in all this and what followed was that I would be having guests for the evening through to the following day. They had managed to contain the disaster of the bad scooter having been delivered to my flat. They had no intention of either returning to their own abodes or being seen entering and leaving mine unnecessarily so we were all holed up together for the night. No one mentioned just how this would impact me. My feelings on that subject remained negative of course. Bruce had clearly been filled in with regards to who I was and my part in all this, either that or he was the least curious creature in the history of forever, beating even me, because he never once asked.

Big Bruce was carrying a battered holdall. It made me nervous. If the gun wasn't bad enough I now imagined instruments of torture or implements to chop me up to make me more easily disposable. Oddly, though Bruce didn't strike me as the perceptive sort he did seem to read my mind just then.

"Food" he said in a surprisingly lightweight voice.

Pete seemed certain to whom this was addressed but automaton me kicked into gear again.

"Shall I prepare something for you?"

It was as if I had spoken magic words and a flying carpet had appeared. I mean a real flying carpet not a 'flying' carpet. A not real, magically levitating rug obviously because they are in fantasy stories. (God story-telling is exhausting). Bruce's dull, doughy face cracked a half smile showing greyish, but thankfully not metal teeth. And also thankfully, I again had something to do that could momentarily distract me from my possible imminent ceasing to exist.

In about forty minutes, Bruce was putting away his second pizza and I was putting away some of the strange goods he'd brought in his bag; microwave burgers already in buns, microwave sponge pudding, microwave chocolate custard, microwave lasagne. I didn't see any need to point out to him while he was still hungry (was he ever in any other state?) that I did not possess a microwave. There was plenty of stuff that did not need nuking. Crisps, biscuits, crisps, fizzy drinks, crisps, packets of chocolate rolls, sausage rolls, crisps and so on. Why was I putting it all away? Why was I, while this brute stranger stuffed carbs down his throat – and I mean down his throat – he had very little use for teeth or tongue as the mess seemed to by-pass both – putting his shopping away neatly in the cupboards in my kitchen, even trying to find appropriate places for things I'd never ever have bought myself? You tell me. I'm just recounting what happened. I'm not a psychiatrist.

Carla was having some strange body language interaction with Pete which alternatively looked like 'fly the fly off and come fly me (to the moon?) Pete was responding with eye-rolls and scowls, the occasional grunt and retreating into the depths of his phone screen. And Frankie was under everyone's feet making train noises, bumping the train backwards and forwards over Bruce's huge feet under the table, a little choo choo train of bright coloured normality in a post-normal world. Bruce didn't seem to mind and I was positively glad of Frankie's happy noises. I continued to clear up. Not that it seemed to matter but it was something else to do.

When Bruce had finished the pizzas and some apple pie I had in the fridge with proper custard and a packet of biscuits and three packs of crisps, some pop and four sausage rolls, he went back into the hall with Pete and there was another exchange of 'terrible travel agent/awful destination' conversation but I didn't catch any of it this time. I was too tired. Carla was talking animatedly on her phone in Italian and Frankie was making more noise with the wooden train which was now being ridden by a brown, smiling, plastic dinosaur. A triceratops, I think.

Then Pete surprised me – and not in a pleasant here's-a-kitten-in-a-box type way - by calling everyone into the living room. I'd emphasise *My Living*room but to be honest, it wasn't feeling like that. Nothing seemed like mine anymore. It had all been properly appropriated.

We trouped in. Even Carla was compliant. Frankie picked up the train engine plus triceratops and brought them too. And Bruce came in last after me. And he did that same thing a moment after he walked into the living room.

"Where's The Telly?"

"She hasn't got one" chorused Pete, Carla and little Frankie. Then they all looked at me as if I was the lunatic, drug-dealing, home-invader.

I do get tired of being made to feel like a crazy person. I just don't see why all this stuff is so compulsory. I mean folk do behave as if it is. And yet everyone is so determined to be 'individual'. 1970s style racists may have been fond of saying 'they' (black people) 'all look the same'. Well folk who spend every day mainlining the crap that pumps out of the TV all seem the same to me. So there. Yes, as you can tell, I wasn't feeling very mature or charitable by this point in proceedings.

AND

If I am anti-TV can you imagine how I feel about the global conspiracy by the capitalist elite to make citizens redundant by inserting current, even more dehumanising technology into every social orifice?

My local Sainsbury has it down to a fine art I must say. At quiet times they put a near-cadaver on one proper till in order to look as if they still care about actual human people and normal interaction while cleverly funnelling shoppers to the self-service tills by making sure that person is usually old Will. When not scanning items at 1 mph after examining each one like he's never seen braeburn apples before or reduced-price natural yoghurt, Will gouges boogers out of his nose equally slowly with his thumb nail or mines for ear wax with the long nail on his small finger.

I fell out with Lidl a long time ago over their no-one on the tills move. You will now find me usually shopping in Aldi even though their bread is not good. That is why I still have to go to Sainsbury and face Will. For the bread.

I tell you – they get you all ways.

But I did not get the impression that Pete had called a team meeting to discuss my views on the current state of Capitalist oppression of the lower orders. I was right.

"Siddown," drawled Pete.

Well, I can tell you I do not like being told what to do in my own home (or anywhere else for that matter) but I sat. I was relieved to sit. I was exhausted. Carla sat next to me on the sofa but not too close. She held herself together and crossed her arms over her pillowy bosom as if touching me might be bad luck. Well, after my experience so far that day – who could blame her. Whether it was the body language or the milk and cookies or the novelty I do not know but Frankie decided the command applied to him too and he jumped up onto the sofa; not onto Carla's lap but mine. There was a long hear-beat of time where Pete looked at Carla who pretended she hadn't been expecting Frankie to land on her knee by re-crossing her legs the other way and ostentatiously closing some app on her phone which made a faint ping. Big Bruce who had worked out that the only chair that would take his weight was the solid oak captain's chair, had wedged as much of his ample buttocks in as would go and leaned forward with his elbows on his knees to stop himself falling out. It was a position that looked as if it would be comfortable for about 3 minutes. He gawped at Pete who clearly decided it was best to ignore the Frankie/Grannie Annie v Carla social faux pas and proceed.

Pete set his stage. Firs he glanced behind him and, while I cannot say for sure, I got the distinct impression he was looking for a mantelpiece so he could pose there and look manly while he delivered what he clearly thought was going to be his Russel Crowe, Gladiator speech. But I don't have a mantelpiece. And of course I could have imagined all that. I have a very active imagination. Pete settled for hooking his thumbs into the waist of his jeans.

Then Pete gave a speech any jaded headmaster 6 months from retirement at a struggling inner city school with a 40% truancy rate would have been proud of. Carla's lips were pursed, Big Bruce looked as if he were trying not to fart (he failed, Frankie giggled) and, even in my I-might-be-dead- tomorrow state I found it hard to concentrate.

If Pete had said 'make your teachers proud, make your parents proud, make me proud' I would not have been surprised. And for all I know – he said something like that. I can't recall. He began along the lines of how none of us wanted the current situation (understatement of the year in my case – the only thing I could want less would be to be stuck in a lift for fifteen minutes with Ann Widdecombe). He moved on to keeping our cool. 'Our' cool, mark you. Bloody cheek! As if I'd chosen to be part of this. Anyway – apparently if we kept 'our' cool things would all work out. By 'work out' – and I'm guessing here – he meant they would end up with lots of money for selling the illicit drugs stash currently residing in the boot of the scooter that was meant to be a pair of earrings in my lean-to/garage/not-a-conservatory.

Pete was 'sure we could do it'. I felt Frankie's head drop onto my shoulder and noticed Carla's little foot flicking up and down impatiently. I didn't want to look at her in case her impatience was with me because I had Frankie or with Pete for being a boring wanker despite being a drug dealer. Bruce shifted his big arse in my lovely captains' chair again and farted again. Sadly Frankie was nearly asleep and in no state to appreciate the moment. Pete droned on. And this next bit may be the hardest of all for you to believe but it is as true as the grass is green. I nodded off again. The room was so warm. The day had been so taxing. Pete was so bloody unbelievably boring; my sofa is very comfortable, Frankie was snuggled in and snoring very faintly which was soothing and soporific.

The next thing I knew was a sharp slap on the cheek. Carla. I know she enjoyed doing it. Bruce was standing and looking incredibly uncomfortable. Pete was positively glowering down at me. Carla snatched Frankie off my knee in a very proprietorial way. He started to half-cry in a not quite awake way. Bruce excused himself and headed – as it turned out – to the bathroom and even though he was able to use the loo with the door shut there was NO disguising what was going on in there. I just hoped no one else was going to need to use the bathroom this side of Halloween.

Frankie woke up properly and started to whimper. Carla looked at me as if it were my fault and started talking to him in some sort of baby Italian then she got up and stomped out into the hall and then into the kitchen and started riffling the cupboards presumably to placate little Frankie with some treat.

Pete turned away, had an absent riffle through my bookshelves. He failed to find anything he'd like to read. I don't keep copies of Marvel comics. Deliberately, he turned back to me, jabbed his finger at me and told me to 'mind what he'd said' as if we were just going to ignore the fact I'd been asleep through most of what he'd churned out. Then he told me to stay right there and stomped out leaving me alone but not as alone as I would dearly have loved to be.

I'd not seen the gun for a while but still nothing had been said about my fate. As far as I know. I had been asleep remember. Tomorrow loomed large and dark in my mind. I tried to put it out of my head because I could see no benefit in dwelling on it. I had not been able to come up with a master escape plan the way you are supposed to if you read the books or see the films. There is always some surprising stash of military grade weaponry that someone accidentally bought once when they meant to get a lawnmower (like going for a scooter when you meant to go for earrings…) and just kept because – well, why not. Or they remember that an old and paranoid relative built a secret passageway under the house and when all the baddies have conveniently fallen asleep leaving the victim unguarded with easily removable ropes – off they pop. No. You will not be astonished to learn. None of these things happened to me. A handy passing SAS troupe did not call in to use the phone, realise I was being held hostage and rescue me. I didn't drug the home invaders all with my secret store of horse tranquillisers (maybe I used to be a vet?). No – I just did as I was told, minute by minute and hoped IT and THEY would all go away.

I can't know if I missed any important information during my second uncharacteristic nap of the day. Had Pete ever said anything worth listening to in his stupid life? I doubt it. But at least he seemed to have concluded that killing me while they still had to spend the night in my flat was probably not such a great idea so what was there for me to do but man-up and try and hold things together a little longer.

As Scarlet O'Hara said at the end of *Gone with the Wind* – "after all, tomorrow is another day".

Chpt 9.

The bad idea

By late afternoon the home invaders had confiscated not just my phone but all the house and window keys. Carla had searched me to ensure I didn't have any spares about my person.

The door from the kitchen to the lean-to could not be accessed from the lean-to side without a key once closed (I'd locked myself out this way many times if I forgot to clip the latch). Even for this mediocre bunch it was only a small step from there to realising that if Carla wanted to re-do her nails and talk on the phone while Frankie was again plonked in front of a screen and 'the men' wanted to smoke and talk macho plans outside but out of sight at the side of the house, the simplest thing to do would be to shut me in the lean-to thingy. Should I develop Houdini talents and attempt to wriggle out of the side window, Bruce and Pete would be there. There was, as yet, no one to hear me shout. There was no way of muscling the door once it was shut and anyhow any attempt would make a huge noise thus alerting the hostage takers. I assume that is what they were and me the hostage. But the tables had fully turned and I felt less like a hostage and more like I was their uninvited and very unwelcome guest.

Being a guest has its own set of rules. I am not especially sociable. Because of this I have, over the years, tried to discern when I am just falling into the rut of the ease of my own company and when it really is that the guest in question is not understanding social rules of engagement. The guests you invite for morning coffee who are still there after suppertime would fall into the latter category. The aunt who invites herself – because she is going to be 'up your way' never mind that 'up your way' is actually 80 miles North and getting her from her previous self-invited visit to yours is an operation of logistical contortion that a time-served military strategist would be proud of - ditto. She then proceeds to spend all the visit telling you the intimate detail of the lives of people she just visited who you have never met and – judging by the 1% you take in – folk you hope never ever cross your path.

When I was a young mum it would be the friends with wrecker kids who you'd dread announcing a visit. The sort where, on learning of their imminent arrival, your own kids would beg you to find hiding places for the things they didn't want smashed to smithereens (whatever smithereens are.)

I had a friend who really put the UG in Unwanted Guest. She was an infrequent but inconvenient visitor after I was divorced. To be fair, a tired, money-strapped, emotionally wrung out single parent playing mum and dad to two children is always going to be on a short string so I'm willing to accept that others may not have had an issue with her behaviour. Although she didn't do what my mum calls (as you already know) a 'proper job', this friend was provided with a nanny and house help by her otherwise horrible husband whose main energies seemed to be spent belittling her in front of other people. Another inadequate male. She would turn up in the evening – and sit in my kitchen and just talk. And talk. And talk. And, perhaps if it had been about something other than nights out and the latest handbag / dress /'d' list celebrity encounter, it might have provided some sort of stimulation or interest to replace much, much needed sleep. I tried all sorts. Letting the central heating go off. Not giving her any more food or drinks. I reduced the 'hmm-ing' and the 'oh reallys' and the 'yes' 'no' 'oh wow' to the occasional nod. She would not go. I realised I was part of her attempt to fill the dark, cold, cavernous time between parties. It wouldn't have mattered if I had lain down on the floor in front of her, closed my eyes and started snoring, she wouldn't leave until she was good and ready.

Well, I felt like an amalgamation of all those people IN MY OWN FLAT. Unwanted. In the way and annoying everyone. That can happen when you find yourself locked in your own lean-to with everyone trying to ignore your existence and with one of those people, a young man with no moral compass, deep down, thinking about the time he will put a bullet in you. And yes it's a contradiction to say he was ignoring me while considering shooting me. Leave me alone.

I presumed he must have a silencer – those things you see films - psychopaths slowly screw them onto the ends of their guns, enjoying the anticipation. Even with absent neighbours and a hedge at the front – there would be no disguising a loud gun shot in this street. And a backfiring exhaust wasn't really a sound you heard much these days.

There must be something I can do. That was what I thought and if there was ever a notion that will get a gal into trouble that surely is it. If there isn't an obvious course of action and you go scratting around in the bins of the mind looking for inspiration, don't be surprised if you come up with a rat.

However, you can understand my motivation for not wanting to be found in the early stages of decomposition with an ugly hole in my head or chest (or both) in a week or ten days' time when my lovely Polish neighbours decided that the strange smell, coupled with the lack of washing appearing and disappearing on the line might be a sign of trouble – without having made an effort. Without having tried to 'do something'.

There was a light but I didn't feel like putting it on. It was gloomy outside, a bit like me, (is that called pathetic fallacy?) but the dull grey which passed for daylight on that unseasonal summer late afternoon was getting in enough for me to see everything essential, including the evil scooter. Pete and Bruce had spent time in here carefully examining the contents earlier. What did they think it was going to do, set off by itself like a scooter version of Herbie, take the drugs to the nearest police station and execute some sort of motorised act of heroism and rescue me in the process? Maybe Bruce was checking it out for size for when he became too large to carry his own weight... You can sense how I was beginning to really resent the presence of the maroon menace in my life.

I had another quick peek in the boot. Yes – the solidly packed, plastic wrapped white stuff was definitely still there. I tiptoed over to the window and by pressing my right cheek against the cool pane could just make out the two men further down the side of the building away from my prison but close enough to have plenty of time to apprehend a tired upper-middle to older-aged woman trying to fit herself through a not particularly large side window.

I was aching all over I can tell you and not a little chilly. The chill must have been internal because even though the day was dull it was not cold. Fortunately, I had on the flip-flops I sometimes use in lieu of slippers though I wished I was wearing socks. I was still wearing the skirt I'd flung on that morning just the first thing I'd grabbed after a perfunctory wash – shower later I'd foolishly thought – plus a long-sleeved jersey top. I couldn't even remember if I'd done my hair – by 'done' I mean tie it up out of the way. But it was up so I must have.

I had a poke around. There wasn't much of interest or anything I didn't remember being there. Nor was there anything that hadn't been there for a long time in its established position (other than the scooter). Just wait until I tell the family how this turned out, I thought. They know what a Luddite I am and swing between amusement and exasperation. But that was another bad thought. So bad that it almost set me crying – which – I think we have established – is not my emotional modus operandi. I took a deep breath and veered away sharply from thinking of what I might do on a tomorrow that might never be fully realised and tried to concentrate on what was under my nose. Well – a small trunk load of cocaine (I'd heard them say that was what it was) was very definitely under my nose – so to speak.

I took another peek. Then, for want of somewhere to sit I manoeuvred onto the scooter seat. I was glad to get off my feet but it was not very comfortable at all. I stood up and had a prod of the seat. It was rather lumpy. Well, if I were a betting woman – which I think we have also established – I am not – I'd have to conclude there was more of the 'aspirational drug' favoured by the likes of Michael Gove secreted about this devil scooter than at first met the eye.

I wondered just how much – in monetary terms – I'd just been literally sitting on. They talked a lot in the news about 'street value' which even I knew had gone down significantly in recent years. So, here is one of the very few examples of the free market economy working if you like. 'They' being news readers who – if they still indulged after their student days – most certainly did not do it on the street.

One thing I'd understood which I felt somehow might be of benefit to me, was that Pete and Carla both appeared calmer now that Big Bruce was here. Not that he was any particular contribution to the brain power and he certainly couldn't be described as the 'muscle' he was more the tower of lard. But, they both seemed to feel I was, now, properly outnumbered and that was why, maybe, I'd seen much less of the gun than before. Frankie was already entirely relaxed in my flat. Well, that was fine. I had nothing against that little sweetie. Carla was tense about something but I wasn't sure it was necessarily to do with me, and Pete was just in a sweat because things had gone so disastrously, ridiculously wrong. But, when were things ever going right if your life was lived his way?

I couldn't help wondering how Pete had got into this. I certainly was having a difficult time with my own starring role. You don't wake up one morning and think – I know – the economy being what it is and me with no qualifications to speak of (or maybe he had – I didn't know) I'll get involved in the distribution of cocaine via old ladies' mobility scooters. It doesn't ring true does it? And how did something that used to be at the very margins of society leach into the middle, the suburban mediocre lives of the low to middle income reality TV watching ordinary folk? Don't worry, that's a rhetorical question.

Nothing else seems to work according to the famous and very popular and misinterpreted Keynesian ideas of supply and demand. But then he wasn't really for the hands-off, let's see how we get on with rampant greed approach which has swamped and bastardised his theories. And our own Adam Smith, son of Edinburgh, would be turning in his grave if he could see how the extreme wealth of the few is underpinned by the state which supports those who could otherwise not live on what they are paid, through benefits. No doubt about it, unlimited credit (debt) and the welfare system pays via our national economic 'trickle up' Ponzi scheme to fill the coffers in the offshore bank accounts and the yachts of the old farts in their golf carts and for the face-lifts of their first wives and the shopping trips of the trophy wives.

I realised I needed to stop that irritating train of thought before my head ruptured, it was barrelling down hill at full steam with broken breaks. Messy metaphor. State of my head.

I went over to the old Belfast sink in the corner. It had a single cold tap which was used for the garden. Usually I approach this square ceramic trough with trepidation because it is a favourite haunt of very large spiders but if I could cope with Pete and the invasion of a druggy version of The Adams Family I could cope with the odd arachnid. Fortunately the sink was spider free – though it needed a clean. I turned the tap which gurgled loudly. Pete's very unwelcome face appeared at the window. He mimed 'WTF are you doing?' I mimed back 'getting a drink of water because you are too ignorant to realise that locking a middle to old aged granny in a lean-to/shed/garage/ not-a-conservatory is cruel and inhuman and if I don't get a drink I will start screaming and you will end up having to shoot me prematurely as – according to Carla – you do everything…' In other words, I showed my cupped hand and mimed drinking.

The water and the unpleasant reminder of Pete's mug at the window focused me a little. However, thoughts of the recreational drugs that are being grown on land that could be growing crops or grazing animals for the families of all the poor but smiling black people we are led to believe are just happy, tootin-dandy delighted to be growing flowers and other cash crops for our supermarkets and fruit that will spend a little time in the dish on the table before going into the save-your-conscience food recycling bin, hadn't entirely left me. As you can see.

I got to wondering if the three adults now making free with my home, took this drug. I'd seen no attempt from any of them to open the stuff that was hidden in the scooter. Maybe it belonged to someone bigger and more dangerous than them. There was always a bigger fish. Or perhaps they had their own supplies. Maybe with the current mess being as it was they were trying to stay on top of things – having rather fallen off things so far – and were abstaining. Doubt it. None of them struck me as abstainers in any way shape or form. Carla from consumerism and delusions, Pete from general coarseness, stupidity and violence and Bruce from – well, food - obviously.

But it didn't necessarily follow, did it, that they took drugs. How would I know – I sort of said to myself. Well, there was no one else to discuss this rather weighty topic with. Maybe not every butcher eats meat, not every bar tender drinks alcohol and so maybe not every drug dealer, drug dealer's big lummox and drug dealer's moll takes drugs themselves. Carla and Pete could be on detox diets for all I knew. She certainly approved of the healthy sausages. Bruce could be a teetotaller. And none of them might ever have touched anything more potent than Bach rescue remedy in their lives.

And I stood and stared at the horrible scooter with its horrible cargo and that was when I nearly could have lost the plot and started yelling and howling and brought forward my demise with a hysterical outburst. I felt a kind of raging madness just below my own surface. I started thinking of all the plots of earth around the globe where people were growing this life-destroying shit. And excuse me but really – are we going to get all overheated about a mild expletive when we accept road deaths by the thousand every year because we are all too lazy to tackle car over-use and while twelve-year-olds openly walk down the street – at least they do here in Edinburgh – smoking genetically altered drugs that will leave them unable to remember their own names by the time they are old enough to vote?. Yes, I was getting in a right lather. It's something I do.

My lovely late partner John – also from Leith – a different part from pathetic Premature Pete I hope – used to talk me down from these emotional precipices – but he's gone. I was on my own. So the thoughts just kept coming. At least I was starting to feel quite warm as I moved agitatedly around the lean-to.

I stubbed my toe and bumped my thigh on something sharp jutting out but barely registered either.

What you may have noticed is that if you get yourself into enough of a funk you can become quite bold. It's the state I end up in when dealing with useless energy companies or train companies or any of the privatised rip-off companies that take vast oceans of public money and don't invest in public infrastructure because Margaret Thatcher hated working class people, her own people and launched the selling off of everything that was theirs by right, into private hands. Well, aren't self-haters always the worst.

I flip flopped over to the window and rapped on it sharply. Pretty quickly two faces appeared somewhat blurred by their very smoky smoke but unmistakably Big Bruce and Premature Pete. They seemed to think leering in at me through my own window was extremely amusing.

"I need to pee." I mouthed. I didn't know to hand signal needing to pee through a window.

"What?" mouthed Big Bruce.

Pete was smirking. I'm fairly sure he knew but just wanted to make me suffer more.

"I need to pee." I yelled.

"Well piss in the sink you silly cow. We're busy and you're not getting out till I say." That was Pete and the two faces disappeared in a cloud of smoky smoke and sniggering.

Bold was turning to furious. Yes – that would be just fine wouldn't it? Me, balanced on the spidery sink and trying to pee and then slipping off and cracking my stupid head on the floor. That would save him a job. But I did need to pee. Necessity, ever the mother of invention, I decided I could do it in the garden bucket and then decant it down the sink without too much risk to life or limb so there I was at some time in the now very late afternoon squatting over a plastic bucket in my own shed/garage whatever, skirt up knickers forward, with two sniggering drug thugs a few yards away very pleased with themselves that they had incarcerated me in my own home while they untangled whatever fine mess they'd got themselves into like a degenerate version of Laurel and Hardy. Meanwhile Carnal Carla and lovely Frankie (you will notice I am like

Donald Trump in that I don't think up stupid names for folk I like. There the similarity ends) enjoyed the comforts of my home.

And that was when I had the really bad idea – the one that led to Premature Pete shooting me prematurely. There are good ideas and bad ones and middling ones and the kind that you dismiss even before they are fully formed. The thing is with most bad ideas the results are not cataclysmic just as most good ideas don't change your life in truly amazing positive ways. It all depends on circumstances.

I have lots of ideas. Some good, some bad, some never fully-formed. But usually the ideas I have do not lead to extreme consequences; ideas don't in the normal course of normal events. Someone having a bad idea while piloting a plane will create a whole different set of circumstances to someone having a very bad idea while waiting for a bus. An idea that occurs to a granny while confused, scared, tired, angry and locked in her own shed with a scooter full of cocaine was never going to be propitious.

Chpt 10.

Stir crazy & charades

I had no idea what was wrong with me. I was wired. I think that is the term. Maybe the events of the day had got me all wound up. Ya think? My heart was racing as if I'd had too much coffee even though I hadn't managed to have any coffee so far that day. I was very tired but just then, didn't feel it and when they eventually let me out of the shed to make the tea I was in a feisty mood, I can tell you.

Bruce started bitching about there being no microwave and him not being able to throw his face at the mountain of ready-to-go crap that could have all been nuked quickly if I had owned said monstrosity. I declared coolly and firmly that I was doing Frankie's tea first. Frankie approved of that so Carla also approved and then I sent fat lad into the living room with a flea in his ear. He looked to Pete for back up but got none from him because Pete wanted a quiet life with Carla and Carla was on Frankie's side and li'll Frankie wanted his tea.

I started banging pots and pans around and rummaging through the fridge-freezer, cupboards etc. while Frankie wove in and out of the kitchen, under the table and back out with a variety of toys he'd found in the small bedroom but always with all or part of the wooden train. Carla sat at the table and watched me in a lethargic kind of way either slouched in the chair or leaning on one elbow with that, now familiar, pouty, sulky expression.

"What's up with you miss sour puss?" I snapped, surprising myself.

And Carla must also have been surprised because she came right out with it.

"I want another baby but it's not happening. I told you" She rolled her eyes and pouted more and looked at me sideways as if she were embarrassed though I didn't get the impression Carla and embarrassment were well acquainted. Maybe she was just checking to see how this news was received or if I had anything to say on the subject. Well – I had plenty to say but wasn't going to go into detail with a child wandering in and out.

"Is there anything *wrong* with either of you?" which as we all know is shorthand for – are either of you infertile because let's face it – if we'd had to go into the list of things that were wrong, in general, with Pete as a human being we'd be there a lot longer than I'd been imprisoned in the shed.

"Not really. We had tests."

"Not really?"

"Sperm count not great but not that low for a Western male."

(Hmmm)

"Well, then you're just not doing it enough or in the right way and I don't mean just the physical act itself." I slammed back fairly brutally. Well, it had been a very trying day and now I was all buzzed up. Perhaps it was the two naps.

For the first time she looked directly at me. Eye contact. Not as some *thing* that needed to be dealt with in order to keep her life ticking along the way she wanted, keep her in salon appointment, holidays and shopping for label goods and her imagined future for Frankie as a latter-day Don Michael Corleone. She obviously hadn't noticed that Pete was no Marlon Brando. Pete definitely saw himself more as Al Pacino but that complicates things. And anyway, Pete was more bit part actor in a Saturday afternoon commissioned radio play where they can't afford actors anyone has heard of or a decent script writer or a decent director or anything other than out-of-the-archives sound effects…

"Tell me." She demanded. Now all on edge, all attention and with a piercing stare and leaning forward as far as the table edge meeting her bursting bosom would allow her.

Just then Frankie choo-choo'd into the kitchen. I looked at him significantly, said, "Later," through pursed lips. Then I turned my back on her triumphantly feeling very put-that-in-your-pipe-and-smoke-it-missy. And proceeded to make the evening meal.

I could feel her eyes on my back but I didn't care. Soon Frankie was at the table tucking in to healthy blended vegetable soup and a nice big slice of thickly buttered bread. Carla watched approvingly, encouraging him although there was no need. Is there anything better than watching a healthy child eat? But Carla's eyes kept flicking to me. I studiously ignored her while I checked on the baking potatoes. I hadn't been expecting long-stay guests (or any at all) and my emergency sausages for unexpected visitors were all used up so I had to make do. We were having baked potatoes – an extra 4 put in just for Bruce with veg chilli but without too much chilli. I didn't imagine poor Pete would cope too well with spicy food though I usually shovel in the chilli for myself. I prepared a green side salad for Carla even managing to find half an avocado which looked very presentable when I'd cut off the bits that had gone brown. Towards the end of the baking time I put in some of the garlic bread I'd found in Bruce's microwave haul because it was possible to oven-cook as well as nuke if you removed all the plastic wrapping and tray.

But as the meal prep progressed, I started to feel the tiredness I knew was there. And I began to experience an unwelcome sense of hopelessness. The full ridiculousness of the situation and the horribleness of my imminent death started poking me, jabbing at me, mocking me until I felt emotionally bruised all over. I tried to tell myself there was always a chance. The police could be on their way right now. Pete might conclude that shooting an old black woman for a bit of cocaine would be disproportionate to the gains to be made from what was – after all – not exactly a tanker load. But I realised that was stupid. This wasn't just about the scooter hooter stash in my shed it was about protecting his whole criminal operation (even I wouldn't go so far as to call it a criminal empire. I'm not delusional) and any previous and future jobs.

And yet if he shot me, the investigation into my death would be far more vigorous than simply an old lady telling the police that she had been locked in her shed by some ne'er do wells. And my whole flat must be a veritable zoo of forensic evidence. They hadn't entered wearing gloves and masks for goodness sake. Then I recalled the conversation about the travel plans. Killing me would give them chance to get away, if they meant to get away in the real sense of the phrase. Me running to the police soon after their departure would not permit a full escape. And anyhow – wasn't I over-thinking everything. Did I imagine they had thought this through? The scooter was here because of amazon Al. Pete was here because of the scooter. Carla was here because Frankie needed a pee at an inconvenient moment and she wasn't the patient sort and Bruce was here to help keep an eye on me until such time as whatever was going to happen tomorrow happened. It was possible that, although Pete wanted to shoot me he hadn't given it the same detailed examination that I was giving it now through my growing headache.

And Bruce chose that moment – possibly in revenge for having to wait more than 5 seconds for food – to slouch against the door jamb grinning and dangling my phone in one meaty paw.

"One of your daughters wants to know if you've fixed the wheel on the spare buggy and Virgin have updated your 'bundle' even though it's a brick phone" And he giggle-laughed as if that was the funniest thing anyone had ever said.

Before I could compose myself I lost my cool and yelled at him,

"You see – they could come here any time and they will when I don't answer and my son in law is an ex-marine" (which he is). But Bruce felt he had the upper hand.

"They really gonna travel from Leeds to Edinburgh tonight you stupid cow? I don't think so." (I learnt later my daughter had also said something about getting the early direct Leeds train next week and asking about the 3 wheel buggy). They will just think you're a stupid old woman who doesn't remember to keep her phone on."

And I don't know if it was just the hiatus or the fact that he'd read my texts or even the truth of that last statement but I could feel everything welling up like a badly maintained drain in a flash flood. The unstoppable fountain. And, as the phrase suggests, I was not going to be able to stop it. And I started to blub. Like a kid who has just been told that both birthdays and Christmas have been cancelled forever – which – in my case they sort of had.

Bruce stopped grinning.

Frankie stopped eating and his little face started to crumple and that was the theoretical smack on the face I needed to control myself. Plus I didn't want another real smack from Carla. Carla stood up, though I've no idea what she was going to say or do because just then Pete – who no one had seen approaching – walloped Bruce on the back of the head told him to stop 'flying around' and ordered him to go back into the living room. Now, bearing in mind this guy was going to shoot me that had to be the most ironic thing that happened in the whole story.

Anyway – I calmed myself down and got back under control. I smiled at Frankie and got him some ice-cream and he recovered, though he watched me for a while and before you knew it the adults (I use that term loosely) were all seated around eating enthusiastically but in rather a subdued manner. By which I mean they ate hungrily but Bruce looked like he'd been given detention, Pete looked like he was finding each second suddenly seemed an hour long and Carla was just distracted.

Frankie buzzed from adult to adult with little gifts of normal human joy – mainly between me and Carla, tasting this and that off our plates and just being a good boy and no bother to anyone. I did notice him yawning and failing to hide it and that got me thinking how the arrangements were going to work out for our impromptu sleepover. And tomorrow? Did Carla and Bruce know Pete intended to shoot me? Would he get them all out into their get-away vehicle and then come back and do me? I do not mean – obviously - 'do' in the way Carla used the word. All of this put me right off the food I was already struggling to eat but everyone else seemed to enjoy it.

Then something occurred that no one had been expecting and as I was beginning to think nothing could surprise me. There was another knock at the door.

Several things happened at once. Bruce grabbed Frankie who did not protest and disappeared into the back bedroom. Pete grabbed me very forcibly, painfully smacked his hand across my mouth with his other arm around my middle then he dragged me backwards into the living room where he simply kept me in a surprisingly strong human vice. Carla whipped out a headscarf from the back pocket of her tight jeans grabbed my reading glasses that were on the kitchen counter and by the time she got to the front door she had covered her hair and put on my specs. And one thing became instantly clear to me, they may seem like a dopey version of The Adams Family but they knew a thing or two about self-preservation and doing what was needed to protect their interests in the real world plus violence was by no means out of the question or even an undesirable option. And just as I had that last thought Pete's arm loosened from my waist and I felt something that was definitely not his penis, sticking into the small of my back.

Oddly, my sense of wanting to cry had completely gone. I wanted to lie down. I wanted to lie down so badly. Tiredness washed over me. Again, it could have been shock but at one point I almost felt I was being kept upright by the hand clamped to my face. Pete must have felt this too because he shoved his knee into the back of my leg. Which was stupid as that nearly collapsed me to the floor but I got the rough non-verbal message and tried harder to support my own weight.

The front door opened and what I heard first was not Carla's voice but a chirpy young man's melody followed by a female voice also young and perky. Oh no. Door chuggers.

"Hi I'm Max." (Max! And you could just tell he was smiling on full beam.)

"And I'm Emma." (Emma – apologetic but also smiling.)

"We were just wondering if we could have a few minutes of your time." (Max – in that how-could-you-refuse-us tone.)

"Have you ever thought of sponsoring research into Fibromyalgia?" (In that I-know-you've-always-wanted-to-do-this-but-no-one-has-ever-given-you-the-chance-by-knocking-on-your-door-on-a-random-evening-while-you-are-trying to-clear-up-the-tea-things tone they dig out from somewhere)

"No." (Carla)

And she shut the door so firmly that, apart from the slam, I could just register it in a slight change in air pressure in the living room. You know – circumstances apart – I could definitely have got to like Carla.

By the time she came into the living room, minus the scarf and glasses, Pete had secreted the weapon, which again made me wonder, although now only in a very vague way, just how much

Carla knew of his intentions. I wasn't fooling myself as to how much she might care even if she did know.

Then Bruce and Frankie came in with my old guitar. Bruce looking a little sheepish I have to say and holding the instrument by the neck but with Frankie dancing around his huge legs trying to strum the strings.

"Granny Annie play." He chirruped. And it may have been my imagination or the brain fog of extreme weariness but again I could have sworn the other adults tensed when Frankie used my name.

Well, I learnt to play the thing at school. Not that exact one. My guitar was stolen at school by – my mum always maintained – one of the teachers- this was a replacement. I learnt to play in the folk group because I really liked the teacher who ran the group. That was pretty much how school went for me. If I liked the teacher I did really well. Fortunately I had quite a lot of decent teachers. But it is a very long time since I played regularly. Most recently I dusted the old thing off to use with a Sunday school group but I guessed – fairly correctly I am sure – that none of the assembled company was up for a rendition of *Jesus wants me for a sunbeam*.

Carla scraped her nails across the strings. Frankie had a go. Bruce twanged a few notes then we fell silent. Pete went out to take a call in the back bedroom and then returned looking no happier.

With a bit of a sit-down I was starting to feel a little better.

"Bed time soon Frankie" said Carla. Frankie wrinkled his nose but didn't seem under the impression that 'soon' meant any time soon so he went back to the guitar which was now leaning in the corner.

"I'll go and wash up," I said and started to get up.

"What's the…" began Carla.

I had a horrible feeling the conclusion to that sentence was to have been 'point' in other words what is the point of washing up if you're going to be dead tomorrow? So maybe she did know or maybe she just wasn't very domestic.

"It's something to do." I said calmly. She flicked her head at Bruce – who was obviously in on the family body language and he followed me into the kitchen and sat at the table eating leftovers while I cleared up, which didn't take very long even though I tried to stretch it out. I also tried very hard not to keep glancing nervously at the door to the shed. And you know as soon as you try not to do a thing that is the very thing you find yourself doing but Bruce showed no interest and Pete was tied up with other matters.

Eventually we were all back in the living room with mugs of tea and that is when I suggested that we play charades.

Bruce perked up from where he was sitting on the floor propped up against the wall under the window – having given up on trying to fit into the captain's chair. But then he caught Pete rolling his eyes and pretended he hadn't thought it was a good idea. But then Carla asked,

"What is charades?" (She said it like Shaaards)

"It is a parlour game – a family game – a game. It helps to pass the time before… er…" I looked at Frankie who seemed very interested "… bedtime."

"We'll do it. It's good to kill…" then it was Carla's turn to be a little lost for words "time."

I have no idea if Frankie had any clue what was being suggested but he certainly cottoned on to the idea that whatever it was meant bedtime would be delayed a little longer and the adults were going to play with him.

And if you think about it, this was a family that naturally seemed to communicate in mime so it was the perfect ice-breaker / time filler. If you consider that the ice wasn't already well and truly broken. If you are of the opinion that if you were facing imminent annihilation maybe the last thing you might want to do is mime *Twelve Angry Men* – which they didn't get or *Avengers* which they did (Frankie had that go and tried to mime *Harry Potter* which consisted of waving around what turned out to be a wand but could have been just a little boy having some sort of sugar induced fit) then all I can say is you have never been in the position I was in so do not judge. Pete refused to join in but seemed to be placated at least that the time was indeed passing – towards the point where he could leave me (my corpse anyway) and get the hell out of there with his moll, his muscle, the boy who definitely was not his and the stash.

I managed to mine the 30%. If you've not heard of it apparently it is inculcated into Marine training that at the point you think you cannot go on or when you are so tired you think you will keel over, you actually have 'another 30%'. Now that may well be complete and total codswallop but the fact that I was still able to get to my feet and explain to these characters from a low budget mobster movie gone wrong – how to play charades - surely proves that if it's not another 30% it is at least 4 or 5 or 6 % because I was still standing.

Then finally it was Frankie's bed time.

Chpt 11.

I blame the parents

I blame the parents - because it's always their/our fault. I mean for the usual stuff. Not focusing enough on the things that matter when they matter and fussing over the things that don't.

But if Carla was doing every conceivable thing wrong, including trying to conceive with an inadequate, aggressive moron like Pete, she was trying to do right by Frankie. In her own peculiar way.

In Frankie you could see all the possibilities, all the over-indulgences and lack of care maybe about some things but he was so good in all the ways that matter. In this instance I blame the parents that Frankie got hurt and of course, it was their fault in all ways.

The bit that will make me smile into eternity is playing chase, up and down the tiny hall. You don't need acres to play – you just need willingness. It was supposed to be bed time and racing about is a no-no. Everyone knows that. You start to calm down. But Frankie had been cooped up all day and had eaten a lot. Even though he looked tired, I could see he needed some physical exertion so we had a run-around. Also, tired as I was, I also needed to work something out before it exploded inside. So we started chucking and chasing a small plastic ball. If I opened the bathroom door at the end of the corridor, that added a couple extra feet. Up and down we went. Pete scowled into the hallway from time to time. Bruce, who I'd established, was definitely a few bricks short of a wall, was eating. Carla, glad Frankie was distracted, was thinking and scheming, everyone waiting. Including me. But the things I was waiting for I hoped would not come. I did not want anyone to go check on the scooter and I did not want to get shot. I didn't even want to get hit with the gun or squashed behind the door or dragged into my own living room with someone's hand clamped over my mouth or kneeing me in the back of the leg. And running up and down was helping me to block things out and also feel less manic.

We chased each other, Frankie shrieked. Pete gritted his teeth. Bruce enjoyed it vicariously. Vicarious was definitely his only exercise. Intermittently he'd laugh, forgetting that his boss was in a bad mood then remember and frown as if someone were pointing a remote emotion control at him and messing around with the buttons.

Frankie laughed and laughed. It was real music but Pete was deaf to the tune. He seemed more irritated than ever but was letting it go maybe because even self-absorbed up as he was he must have known the kid would sleep better if he got rid of some energy both nervous and physical. The atmosphere was terrible. Each time we hurtled past the open living room door it was like passing a cold grey chasm – entirely different to the party atmosphere in the corridor. Then the door was shut firmly from inside.

Unexpectedly, a very out of breath Frankie stopped, turned, yanked down his trousers and pants pointed his willie at me and guffawed in a victorious kind of child's roar/laugh. I can't tell you the control needed – or where it came from – to smoothly switch to the important serious-but-not-cross face, level my breathing and say, in calm adult tones – 'now, Frankie – we only need to get that out if we need a pee pee' – and then avert my eyes while he pulled up. What I wanted to say was 'kid you got great timing and a fantastic sense of humour'. You had to conclude, absolutely, Pete wasn't his bio-daddy. He wasn't even his 'real' daddy in the way good step-dads are. In my view it was unlikely he ever would be.

That was when the arguing started from the living room. You could have been mistaken for thinking someone just whacked up the volume on the TV but – yes – there wasn't one. Frankie froze and so did I. If he'd been a mouse I'd have said his ears pricked up and his nose started twitching. Certainly his antennae were searching for important clues – the main one being 'is this something I should be concerned about?' I just stood like an idiot listening too. There were peaks and troughs of decibels as if both were trying to make some concession to circumstances, then remembering the adjoining properties were (or had been) empty. Then maybe realising they needed to be careful anyway the battle reverted to muted but aggressive sniping with lots of 'fly's flying.

And the thing that caught my attention was that Carla gave as good as she got. I knew she was feisty so I'm not sure why that astonished and pleased me but it did. Then I remembered my own reaction when the husband was having a rage, me trying to be composed while he variously ran through the dictionary of expletives, banged about like a giant toddler having a tantrum or lied, wheedled and cajoled to ensure he got his way, with me always and ridiculously trying to be civilised for the sake of the children. No wonder my eldest had no respect for me by the time she was a teenager. Should I have been more like Carla?

A woman friend who I no longer see had a husband who would orchestrate a nasty scene if he wanted to go off to do something for himself when he ought to have been helping with family stuff. That would allow him to, for example, slam on the brakes at a junction, bang out of the car, and stomp righteously off up the street after screaming some abuse, leaving her with one little boy sobbing and another glaring at her with a hatred akin to concentrated acid. She then simply climbed over into the driver's seat amid the hooting horns, howling children and other gesticulating drivers and headed off to wherever it was they were going that hubby had never wanted to go to. He, meanwhile, would be on the way to wherever it was he always intended to go to. Carla wouldn't have put up with that.

I was just running over this reverie when Bruce eased out of the back bedroom door where I hadn't known he was, with remarkable agility for a bloke his size. Then he pointed at Frankie and mimed hands palms-together by his cheek leaning on his left shoulder, eyes closed. Even in my exhausted state I could get that. Both Frankie and I were happy to have something to do that took us away from the now dull old hall and portal to parental hell - living room door.

With the bath running, the noise of the gushing tap and the chugging of the water in the system was very welcome. Soon the bathroom began to fill up with steam and Frankie had found the bath toys and was chucking them in. Bruce was standing guard in the doorway. I told him where to find PJs for Frankie. He only hesitated a moment before concluding that there was no risk in this, the bathroom window was high enough up to be more than a challenge - and off he went.

And there we were shortly afterwards - another entirely normal vignette to any outside observer but in a completely abnormal set of circumstances. Frankie splashed, I knelt by the side of the bath and Bruce sat on the toilet seat actually looking more comfortable than he had since he arrived. He kept swiping at the screen of his phone. Probably he was looking at different apps or maybe he was trying to clear the steam. And somewhere in a galaxy far, far away Pete and Carla slugged it out. For a brief moment I had a vision of sexy Carla with her red mouth turning into some sort of femme fatal vampire from one of those fabulously dingy 1940s black and white horror movies you can watch on YouTube and tearing out Pete's jugular then marching off into the night with Frankie and everything going back to normal. Or wrestling the gun off him and shooting him and everything returning to normal. Or him having an aneurism and everything returning to normal. Or her being visited by an angel then telling Pete she was pregnant and him going crazy and shooting everyone. Oh dear. That got a bit out of hand. I snapped out of my little side-track to find Frankie staring at me with a blue and white plastic shark in one hand and a green boat in the other, his mouth a little 'o'. Bruce was also staring at me, frowning. I ignored Bruce and smiled at Frankie with all the strength I could muster. His mouth turned up into a smile, his eyes joined in and he continued playing.

Bruce hauled Frankie out of the bath for me as I hardly had strength to stand. Then, with Frankie towelled and in my grandson's pyjamas we were all back in the hall. There was the briefest second of hesitation while all three of us, I'm sure, contemplated whether Frankie should be taken to the living room to say goodnight to his parents and we all decided at the exact same moment it was a bad idea and turned into the little back bedroom instead. Also, I realised, all three of us had accepted that it was normal for Bruce to accompany me and Frankie wherever we went while Carla and Pete were otherwise occupied. The things the human brain can bend to given enough motivation.

It was beginning to feel as if someone kept stopping and starting a film with me in another set piece each time the camera began to roll again. I cannot say I have detailed memories of getting Frankie into bed or choosing books. I certainly have no recollection of Bruce settling himself in the corner opposite the door and looking as comfy as he had on the loo seat. Maybe at his size he often had to use the floor and a wall as a makeshift sofa. But eventually he'd find getting up a chore I would guess. I do, however, remember thinking that tomorrow there would be an awful greasy mark on the wall where he rested his head and then reminding myself that thinking about tomorrow was not helpful.

The row ebbed and flowed. Sometimes the screaming and shouting was full on other times it was like two dogs snarling and growling at each other in an alley. Frankie seemed to have decided to ignore it and focus on the stories. I could see he was very tired but also a bit wired, not unlike me and I reckoned if I could get him into a good long story and just keep the words flowing he'd sink away into sleep however hard he was fighting it.

I'd finished the second book, Frankie's eyes were drooping and it was time to go for the long one when I risked a murmured question to Bruce.

"Does this happen a lot?"

And, slick as you like and without looking away from his phone screen Bruce replied,

"She wants another baby real bad and he's stressed and I think she's ovulating but – ye know – it's difficult to *perform* (he waggled his head when he said this) when you're struggling with self-esteem and work pressures. She reckons she can't get pregnant because he doesn't give her full orgasms and he says she intimidates him in bed. Nuff said."

Good heavens, Pete thought he was Al Pacino and Bruce thought he was Oprah bloody Winfrey.

I mimed reading the final book to Bruce and flicked my head in the direction of the living room in a way that was meant to indicate that he should tell Carla and Pete to take it outside. He hesitated for another moment and I didn't even try to work out what he might be contemplating – whether I could be left in the bedroom where there was a good sized window albeit that the locks had been checked and the keys taken. Really my little flat was turning into a proper fire hazard (another bad thought). Or maybe he was anticipating the reception he'd get from Pete and Carla. But whatever he concluded – that it would all be easier if we could get Frankie to sleep or what - I do not know. He got up without too much difficulty, went next door and a minute later he was back and a few moments after that I could hear the front door being opened and closed and locked from outside and the arguing noises ceased.

I started *Georges Marvellous Medicine*, slowly and steadily, holding the book so that Frankie could initially see the illustrations without lifting his head and I carried on reading long after he'd closed his eyes.

I could have shut my own and just lay down on the floor right there. The overhead light was off and just the small bedside lamp created enough glow to read by. It was fortunate – and wasn't I owed some good fortune? - I knew all the stories almost by heart and the font was clear because I'd no idea where my reading glasses got to after Carla used them in her disguise. I could have pulled the spare blanket off the end of the bed and stretched out and forgotten all about everything and what was going to happen tomorrow and what might happen tonight if I had the kind of luck I'd been having all day and how I got into this horrible mess and so on and so on but that was when I discerned a very strange sound. It was like the rumble of a small outboard motor. I glanced over to the corner, barely daring to pull in a breath and saw that Bruce's eyes were closed, his big head had fallen forwards and his huge hands, still clasping his phone, were slack in his lap.

Terrible.

Could anything worse possibly have happened? This meant I had to do something. I had to try and save myself. I had to try and save myself for the very simple reason that a real practical opportunity had presented itself. Frankie was properly, deeply asleep; I could tell by the way he was breathing. When kids are asleep like that you could let a firecracker off at the end of the bed and they would not wake up. And Bruce was asleep. How deeply I had no way of knowing. What I did know was that the responsibility was all mine now. Both Carla and Pete were out of the flat thinking I was being supervised by Big Bruce. I suspected they went to the car to *Carry on Arguing* as it was pretty dark outside.

Bruce doesn't – as far as you know – have a gun, I told myself. It didn't help. He was very big and now that I had the responsibility to try and save myself he suddenly didn't seem like a big lump of lard anymore – but something like *The Predator*, in the original movie with Arnold Schwarzenegger. Vicious murdering alien or not – he was still more than twice my weight and over 6 ft. But he was ASLEEP. And that meant that any self-respecting hostage not tied up or gagged or dead had to try and save herself. I really wished I'd just stretched out on the carpet and not looked over into the corner but it was his fault for snoring. Snoring was supposed to indicate deep sleep but I knew that was rubbish. My lovely partner used to snore and he could get up in the night, go for a wee, get back into bed and be snoring before he'd made a dent in the pillow.

I had to move. There was no other way out of this.

As I stood up, all nerves tingling now and feeling very falsely wide awake, my knees creaked. It sounded, to my ears, like the amplified howling of a never oiled, 500 year old, rotten wooden door on rusted hinges. Bruce did not stir. I didn't know whether to climb over Frankie, who would probably not wake up, in order to avoid having to go anywhere near Bruce or just to walk around the end of the bed.

I really needed to pull myself together and maybe think a bit less, at least until I got out of the bedroom. I glanced down at my feet. At some point, possibly when I was running up and down the hallway with Frankie, the flip flops had come off. That was good. Breathing with my mouth open and my eyes on stalks I crept around the bed and got to the door in what felt like three days.

I stuck my head out into the hallway then looked back at the huge lump in the corner of the room. No movement.

I darted into the kitchen, all sleepiness gone. I checked the windows. All locked. The door to the lean-to was not locked but I knew the outside one was, ditto the window in there. I hurried back into the corridor and, a little hesitantly, proceeded to the living room. I'd heard things go quiet and the front door open and close but I had no definite confirmation that they both went out. There was no one there but a quick glance at the window was enough to show me that all the keys were gone from here too, where I usually leave at least one in a lock. If it came to smashing a window I really should just do it. Last chance and all that but the odds of that waking Bruce were too high to try without checking all else. Also, the risks of serious lacerations getting through a broken window in my state were not small and the likelihood that Pete wasn't that far away and might decide that I'd been enough trouble and now that Frankie was asleep would be as good a time as any to 'do' me (in the other way) was also strong.

My last chance was the bathroom window. Being higher up, maybe they hadn't locked it? Perhaps they thought it was not only too high for an old woman (I no longer felt anywhere near middle-aged) but too small and maybe I was fantasising but a desperate woman should have a go. The bathroom meant passing the open bedroom door where Bruce was sitting directly opposite the gap. No worries, I was, after all, heading to the bathroom so there was an obvious excuse handy. I'd just say I needed a pee. I know there is a lot of needing to urinate in this story but maybe I am redressing the balance for all the stories where no one ever needs the loo.

I got to the bathroom and found I really did need to pee. The sensation came on so abruptly and so desperately it was like having instant cystitis. There was nothing for it; I didn't want my bladder to go as I was half way through an escape. I yanked my skirt up and my knickers down and sat and of course it wouldn't come. I willed myself to concentrate on my bladder and not on either escape or getting shot just for the next few seconds and finally relieved myself. Knickers up quick, skirt down and I'm sorry to say that I did not wash my hands.

It would have been better if I'd been wearing trousers but hey ho. I lowered the loo lid but obviously did not flush. Before checking the window, I pushed the bathroom door too but not shut. Then I climbed onto the narrow, low level cistern and reached for the window. And good lord almighty it was not locked. I felt a little faint at that and had to get down.

After taking a couple of steadying breaths, I climbed back up and turned the latch quietly and slowly. I could already imagine making my way along the gardens at the back and surprising some poor neighbour with a desperate knock on their window. Which was only poetic justice; all sorts of undesirables had been knocking on my front door. Or maybe I'd just keep going until I was much further away, maybe in another street before risking stopping to ask for help. I still hadn't worked out how I was going to drag myself up to the level of the window but I suspected one of the stools in the kitchen might do it if I balanced one on the seat lid and I was also fairly sure that if I didn't worry too much about landing on the other side, I could let my head and shoulders through and let the rest just fall. It was grass under the window. So, I got down to sneak back to the kitchen. And that was when I heard voices and the key in the sash-lock of the front door.

I thought I was actually going to have a heart attack. Bruce must have woken up too because I heard that big lummox groan and shift himself.

With my heart hammering so violently I thought it would rupture, I got back up on the cistern and closed the window as quickly and quietly as I possibly could. Then, all too quickly I heard,

"Where the fly is she?" from Pete in the bedroom in a super not-happy tone of voice.

"Eh - what?" from Bruce just as both my feet made contact with the bathroom floor and the door was shoved open. Carla stood there with one well plucked, raised eyebrow which clearly said 'Hey, just what the hell were you up to old woman?'

Swallowing my panic heroically and controlling my breathing as best I could and trying to look tired rather than panicked I simply said,

"Wee."

Bruce was now looking, not a little relieved, over Carla's shoulder. Pete forced himself between them both, which was no mean feat and lifted up the toilet lid and regarded the yellow, clearly fresh contents of the bowl and let the lid slam down. He looked up to see if the window was shut which it was then he grimaced at me but said nothing.

Then, calm as you like – and I think I was so terrified, the calm settled on me like ice in a hailstorm – I flushed the toilet, quickly washed my hands, watched by Carla and Bruce, said "excuse me" and walked out of the bathroom and into the kitchen.

In the kitchen, shaking and clammy, I braced myself over the sink thinking I was definitely going to vomit.

Chpt 12.

Carla wants a baby (the sex bit)

By the time *Mary, Mungo & Midge* followed me into the kitchen I'd managed to splash my face with cold water and regain enough composure to convince anyone who didn't know me that I was as fine as a tired, abused, pistol-whipped granny hostage could be and in no way suffering the effects of a desperate and failed escape attempt forced on me by Big Bruce's snoring.

If you don't get that MMM reference by the way, it's from back in the day before so-called children's television became a mess of pointless hysterical noise, psychedelic animated hyper-activity and lunatic steroidal storylines aimed only at training children to watch mindless reality TV in later life. And the less feverish ones are sickly. If I ever meet *Pepper* flying *Pig* I'll go back to being a meat eater. And since the Post Office was sold off to oil sheikhs and other shady characters dirt cheap, you can hardly expect *Postman Pat* to have stood the test of time.

There was no doubt in my mind, I had most definitely used up the fabled 30% of reserve energy, resilience and simple ability to *Carry on Standing* so I cannot explain how I was able to get through the next few hours. Maybe, once you've used up the 30% you didn't know existed, that in turn has its own 30% and that in turn has its own 30% multiplying down into infinity like a mad reverse Fibonacci.

Yes, anyway – this is the sex bit by which I mean the kind of sex you got at school (no, not the girl and boy who were a bit ahead of everyone else behind the bike sheds – when they weren't being used for smoking – the sheds not the boy and girl…) I mean where babies come from and how. If you were expecting lengthy descriptions of lascivious liaisons – tough. If you wanted someone swinging knicker-less from chandeliers, I can't help but you can get that pantomime sex pretty much anywhere else. There is an epidemic of it.

And if you are thinking that's a bit of a cheat well tough again. Sex sells, apparently, which is why young women were always draped over cars or fellating chocolate bars in the 1970s and 80s and why I put it in the title. I mean not to me. I'd be as likely to fork out for a copy of *50 Shades of Grey* as I would be to eat a three-day-old dog pooh sandwich. A reading buddy reckoned if I was going to slate it I shouldn't unless I'd read it. But as I said then, I've never eaten a dog pooh sandwich but I'm fairly sure I know I wouldn't enjoy it.

I could have called my account of this sorry incident 'Grannie Gets Clobbered'. Would you have bought that? Or 'Twenty Four Hours at Granny's Flat.' Or 'What Happened after I'd Bottled the Beetroot.' Come on.

Sex and violence does of course have a nobler literary pedigree. Frankly, if you removed the sex and violence from Shakespeare you'd be left with Mills & Boon on a bad day. Although – if statistics are to be believed – nowadays there is more looking at it and reading about it than there is actually doing it in wealthy Western nations. And that was part of Carla's problem. Plus – the prospective father wasn't called 'Premature Pete' just because he doesn't know when to smack a granny over the head with the butt of a gun.

Carla led the mismatched trio into the kitchen, sat down opposite me and indicated with her chin that I should sit down on the side of the table by the sink. Thus I had, not only her but the table between me and any means of escape plus an even clearer sense that she play acted this sham for Pete's ego.

Pete took out his gun, waved it at me and placed it ostentatiously on the counter by the door just to the right side of the now seated Carla then crossed his arms and leaned against the door jamb watching me. She rolled her eyes, for my benefit I suspect, as if she'd never seen anything as ridiculous and silly as a gun. Whether this was supposed to make me feel more relaxed I don't know. Though, it did suggest there was just the one gun. My word, how we adjust. The idea that I would ever think 'just' one gun was preposterous and funny.

Then Bruce, doing his best to look like the mean mother muscle – but succeeding only in looking like a very large naughty boy who very nearly got caught with his big paws in the cookie jar and who knows he had a close call, lumbered over to my side of the table. Without making eye-contact, he squeezed, with great difficulty, between the back of my chair and the sink, took my left arm roughly and cable tied it to the back of the seat.

This meant I had to sit slightly side on to the table but at least I was sitting down again and the three cable ties were close fitting but not cutting into me. He obviously meant to do the same to my left ankle but simply could not find room to bend down on that side so forced his bulk back behind the chair and secured my right ankle instead. Then he stood up sweating and red in the face and exited with as much dignity as he could muster – which was none. Pete turned his attention to me, jabbing his finger.

"The Guys have got stuff to do - right. We're going out and you are going to behave. Capice?"

I nodded demurely although even that movement was starting to set off waves of queasiness to the accompaniment of a quite spectacularly hammering headache. Who in the name of re-hashed slush movie scripts from the 1990s was writing the bollocks in Pete's head? He departed with what he obviously imagined was a macho sneer but which made him look as if he had infected haemorrhoids.

"He's not a bad person." This was Carla's opening gambit. You have to hand it to this old bird, I managed not to snap back with a sarcastic 'you could have fooled me'. They say sarcasm is the lowest form of wit – well shoot me – no don't actually – I love a bit of sarcasm. It's often hilarious although more than any other form of humour it relies on context. She continued, clearly thinking she was buttering me up but there was no need. I was happy to tell her anything she wanted to know that might put Pete in a better mood.

"He wants to go straight and be the normal living guy but the capitalist system – you know…"

I nodded sympathetically but not over doing it. Nor did I mention that my own attempts to thwart the capitalist oppressors, global elites and Russian oligarchs did not involve drug running. I resisted pointing out that in the end, a well penned letter to the national press and a stern refusal to be coerced into a zombified automaton existence by the supermarkets by not using self-service tills might have a more positive effect than providing the mindless, be-suited mega-consumers with their aspirational drug of choice at market prices.

She continued.

"He's already invested some money in bitcoin" (oh boy) "and after just another couple of contracts" (she had the decency to look away from me when she said 'contracts' – it wasn't as if he was building a hospital) we're going to get a good place in a good area for Frankie. Not in Britain obviously because of flying Brexit. My Frankie, he deserves somewhere decent – not run with racists yes?" This tipping a nod to my colour did make me feel a sneaking scintilla of positive to her which may have something to do with the two incidents of blatant racism I experienced the day after the referendum. As an average, once or twice a year would have been about right. Two in two days was a definite and unwelcome personal upsurge.

She produced an e-cig and started filling the small kitchen with the stink of chemical plug-in air freshener which added beautifully to the headache and wiped out her plus point. And, when finally there was a sensible pause in the 'Pete is a misunderstood serious businessman' crap, I pulled the conversation to where she wanted it.

"But you can't get pregnant?" plus what I hoped was a sympathetic face but if my ability to make the face of choice was anywhere like Pete's, I just looked like an old woman who had seen better days, needed a bath, a very large mug of tea and to lie down for a week.

Her shoulders dropped and she let out a huge plume of whitish smoke, blowing it very courteously to one side as if that was going to make the slightest difference in such a confined space. It did, however, draw my eye over to the kitchen door that led to the lean-to and I didn't want to think about that so I pushed on a little hurriedly.

"And you've both been tested you said…"

"Him, not me. I got Frankie before I met him."

(Of course you did.)

A whole army of questions marched across my poor aching brain; where did you meet? Why the hell did you go out with him? What possessed you to bring a dangerous, deluded idiot like this into Frankie's little life? And so on. But I bit them all back.

"And his test?"

"They *said* he's ok. Apart from bit low spermatozoa…"

The way she emphasised that word suggested she either wasn't convinced about the tests and Pete's fertility or she had her own doubts about whether he was *ok* – I mean in all ways – sane, sensible, a fully formed human being. And she'd have to be mad not to have those doubts. But here she was, sitting opposite, with me strapped to a chair and a gun at her shoulder that she pretended she found distasteful but which Pete had been happy to leave with her and, I noticed for the first time, with a bulky, short barrel next to it which, I assumed was a silencer. Not good.

So – we had the conversation

"How long have you been trying?"

"18 months – give or take"

"How long did it take to catch with Frankie?"

"I was pregnant about 5 seconds after he looked at me (I didn't ask who the 'he' was obviously.)

"How long does he – ya know…?"

"Depends."

"On what?"

She gave quite an extensive list which included what he had eaten that day and whether his football team was doing well, which I thought was very insightful.

"Do you usually have time to – you know…?"

"If I'm already in the mood – he can be quite… er – passionate – driven – animalistic – quick! You think that's important? One of my girlfriends said it's because he doesn't make me come enough. Is this a problem?"

Good lord – I thought – she's been canvassing opinion. I wonder if Pete knows about that. I could not imagine it would go down well… but what I said was –

"My dear – you are not the Conservative party – there is no need for you to 'come together when the fighting is over'" but she didn't' get my little joke so I continued. "There is one school of thought that it makes a difference, makes the woman more receptive, but if it were important only loving consenting couples would ever get pregnant and we know that is far from the case. So…"

And on we went through all sorts of intimacies that would have made a midwife blush. Ok, not many midwives – they are a pretty tough bunch.

"What position, usually?"

"8*RJ@"

"Hmm, and how often?"

"~£&)>|&%"

"I see. Less when he's 'working'?"

"$(+=){J^EO _"

"Ok. And is there anything he particularly likes to do in bed?"

"+~#x!)9>*"

"My goodness, you must be very flexible."

"I do yoga."

"Marvellous."

And so on until my head was spinning one way while the room went in the other direction.

"Ok – so, this is what I suggest, try on your knees with your bum in the air and down on the elbows when trying to conceive and with the end of the bed slightly raised. And for goodness sake stop all this – we have to have sex because I'm ovulating (woops, I hoped I'd not given Bruce away there) it's not encouraging for a man (especially one with a fragile ego like Pete) and may just reminds him he is – you know – not Giacomo Casanova." And, presumably because she's Italian, she got that reference and laughed like a drain. We continued a while more. The normal women chat was soothing and eventually concluded with "Obviously try to keep alcohol to a minimum (I didn't mention drugs) and no heavy meals and try (especially for a moron like Pete) to get him in the mood as often as possible without letting on that is what you are doing."

"Really, that's it?"

"Yes," (in your case anyhow, I thought)

I could have gone into the physiology and the psychology of why it works but there was no need – she wasn't interested in the why of it just that it might work.

And don't you go getting the idea that all this is from personal experimentation. I got pregnant easily and what I may have lacked in youthful sexual exploration, I've made up for in the fact that I listen and observe and pay attention to what is going on and what is being said around me by my women friends. Writers do, you know.

Then we talked some more, because Carla wanted to, about the best ways of getting Mr macho in the mood and not banging on (no pun intended) about actually getting pregnant and trying to make it seem like the sex was his idea blah blah blah. Dear lord she looked like she wanted to put the new info into action right away.

And her looks were not deceiving.

The unwelcome sound of approaching male voices and the front door being unlocked caused Carla to sit back in her seat and morph her facial expression into one of distant disinterest. It was like a curtain coming down on a play rather before the end. Just in time I picked up the cue and slumped back in the chair trying to look like a hostage and not someone who had, a few moments earlier, been discussing Pete's shortcomings. Again – no pun intended.

Pete looked as if he'd had some sort of machismo fix rather than a druggie fix. He swaggered into the kitchen with Bruce following and also looking as if he'd taken a short partially-effective course in how to transform from *The Blob* into the semi-dangerous side-kick. Bruce stood blocking the door behind Carla with his black leather jacket on, which was making him sweat profusely and the bag he'd originally arrived with. Pete planted his knuckles on the table and leant forwards in his 'listen carefully, I'm in charge' pose. He stared down at me in what I suspect he hoped was a searching, brooding and threatening manner. And he might have succeeded if what was going through my head wasn't 'please, please, please do not decide to go into the lean-to. Not now. Not just now. Please.' But as we were all playing pull-a-silly-face I hoped mine simply exuded weary resignation. Weary I could muster. Resignation I didn't have to fake. It was 'guilty conscience' I was trying to keep off my face.

I'd not known Pete very long but even I realised he was about to do another dreadful audition for a bad gangster movie.

"Ok. Listen up." By which I presume he meant 'listen'. We're not American. He continued.

"No one wanted things to turn out like this (understatement of the day as far as I was concerned) but we're just going to deal with it. (If he says 'capice' again I'll scream) "Ok?"

Carla nodded, Bruce nodded so I nodded. Pete carried on. *Carry on Pete.*

"I've had a looong hard day and I'm going to bed."

I could not help glancing at the clock on the wall and was surprised to see that it was just coming up to 11.15pm and it had, indeed, been a very tiring day. But the unfairness of him claiming to be tired and, presumably intending to sleep in my lovely double bed with the very comfortable mattress brought another unaccustomed attack of the weepies. I managed to swallow them down by staring at the table where my one free hand was clenched in a pointless fist.

"YOU…" he yelled and banged the table really making me jump and look up at him. It did not startle either Carla or Bruce, "…you are going to behave. In a minute Big Bruce is going to cut you loose and take you into the living room where you will be firmly secured. Bruce is going to sleep on the floor with intermittent alarms on his phone. Try any funny business and it will be more than a tap on the head ok?" Well, as far as I was concerned, albeit he hadn't hit me as hard as he intended, the first one was a lot more than a tap but I nodded, no longer needing to pretend to look miserable and cowed. "You." This time he pointed at Carla and jabbed his thumb at the door. Bruce stepped back into the corridor to let Carla pass and the little minx did a marvellous impression of going grudgingly into the bedroom while pouting and swinging her 'fly me to the moon' hips in a very provocative manner.

Thus hugely satisfied with his manly performance, Pete turned and strode out of the kitchen stopping only to reach and grab the gun, turn and stare significantly at me and then proceed into my bedroom after Carla.

Clearly forgetting that I was cable tied to the seat Bruce tried to emulate his lord and master and waggled his hand at me in a 'get up' motion. At least it would have been a 'get up' signal if I'd been a border collie. Suddenly he remembered and drew out something that looked a bit like a Swiss army knife. Exhausted to the point of torpor as I was, I barely had the time or the available brain cells to wonder if he was going to kill me nice and quietly now that Carla and Pete had gone to procreate, before he was sawing through the cable ties at my ankle followed by the ones securing my arm. Once my limbs were released I realised I'd become very uncomfortable and it wasn't initially easy for me to stand up. Fortunately, Bruce was not as impatient as Pete. In fact he behaved as if he had all the time in the world.

Eventually I was stable on my feet and even more eventually we were both in the living room with me sitting, thankfully, on my nice comfy Parker Knoll sofa which I got off Gumtree for a real bargain. These days everyone seems to want those bulky things that look like beds and take up all the floor space in the living area. As my lower back rested against the beautifully shaped base of the chair rise, I could have sung out the Hallelujah Chorus. Then Bruce produced something very surprising indeed, out of the bag that had previously held all the microwave faux-food. A chain, approximately 6 foot long with a cuff at each end so it looked like over-extended handcuffs.

"One end for you and one for me. That way no funny business and the boss can get some sleep."

Clearly, another escape attempt, which they obviously suspected, was one kind of coitus interruptus my captors were not going to risk.

"And," Bruce continued, "you might get some rest. That would make you feel better wouldn't it? Things don't have to turn out bad you know."

Then I had to settle back in the chair and close my eyes because I was so, so, so tired and stupid Bruce sounded as if he meant what he said and also as if he wanted it to be true and that, more than anything, was too much to endure.

Chpt 13.

Nightmare

You would think that with Pete and Carla rutting in the next room and Bruce snoring in the corner and the ankle cuff digging and the chain to the cuff around his wrist clinking occasionally as one or other of us changed positions, I would not sleep. You'd be wrong. Plus I'd had two surprise naps but you'd still be wrong. I felt as if I'd given birth to a 10lb baby, which I've done, after running a marathon, which I haven't. I ran two half marathons in my youth but many months apart so I don't think you can just tack them together and say you ran a marathon. It's like an old minister of mine who added up all the sermons he'd written and happily told me it was the same as having written a book. Fool.

Discomfort or not, I was instantly, deeply, deliciously unconscious. When I think of the years of insomnia I've suffered. If I'd only known that all you need is a horrible young man to start your day off by whacking you in the temple with a gun butt after another chump has wrongly delivered a drug scooter to your home and then set up camp with his dysfunctional family, imprisoning you in your own shed/lean-to after you provided free childcare and making you pee in a bucket, I could have saved myself many sleepless nights.

After what may have been a very brief time, however, I shot bolt upright, eyes wide in the almost complete dark with another pain to add to the growing inventory; this time in my neck. I also had a very dry mouth. I simply sat not knowing where I was, barely who I was, just feeling panicky and a bit sick and with a headache that felt lazy, heavy and settled, in what I would call forever after, if there was such a thing, a 'Bruce headache'.

I got a bit of a fright when the dark mound on the floor near my feet, morphed gradually into human shape and grunted and rolled on its side. Then I remembered. Everything. Fast as my recollections came I tried to blot them out. I just did not have enough energy to deal with them all. I tugged carefully at the leg with the cuff around the ankle. There was quite a lot of play, what with Bruce lying in a heap towards me. I manoeuvred as cautiously as I could, hotching over to the right on the sofa and lifting both legs very, super carefully up onto the seat. And if you think this was the start of some new master plan to escape you are mistaken again. The only thought my poor head had room for amongst the headache was getting a little more comfortable and maybe getting some sleep – which seemed the only relief on offer from this nightmare.

I did – as humans are want to do – try even in my exhausted, semi-comatose state – to convince myself that I'd not given in. With a little sleep maybe some amazing solution to all this would come to me out of the blue. The reality was I wasn't thinking that far ahead. I was simply hoping the chain would not make a noise and I could get my legs up onto the sofa and lie down. Even though my flat tends to stay wonderfully cool even on the hottest day I was more than warm enough, perhaps a little too warm. I suspect Bruce acted like a human radiator. Maybe he could be an answer to the energy crises.

And then, there I was, horizontal. My back and shoulders stopped screaming and even my head eased off just slightly. Then with the idea in-for-a-penny-in-for-a-pound I hotched again, onto my side and pulled my knees up a little pressing my back into the back of the sofa with my arm under my head and if I've ever been in a more comfortable position ever in my life I cannot say I remember it.

Without even time to consider if this was best use of a moment when Bruce was asleep, Frankie was asleep and the rutting had temporarily ceased, to try and escape, darkness descended.

I dreamed a horrible dream. It started, obviously, with me pickling beetroot but in the boot of the scooter. The problem was I couldn't contain the vinegar in the boot of the scooter long enough to get the beetroot in and shut the lid. It was dark and I knew if I could only get the window open the fresh air would help me think and the light would come in. I have no idea why the light could not come through the window in the ordinary way – it was a dream.

For some reason, in the dream, I knew I'd been doing this task for a very long time and would keep on doing it until I died. No one knew I was doing it and no one cared. No one apart from me even liked pickled beetroot that much and that made me sad. Suddenly, the door from the kitchen opened and Pete was standing there naked, except his penis was actually a small gun. I bolted out of the door which turned into an open window so that on the other side I fell to the ground. I started running but it was suddenly full dark outside. I tried a route I thought I knew but there was a huge mound in my way which turned out to be a human tummy with no head or arms or legs and I had to climb over it to escape. I started trying to climb but the more I clambered and scrambled across the vast doughy mound the larger it got and my feet and hands sank in. Then I was racing down a street I did not recognise with Pete fleeing beside me instead of behind me – no longer chasing me but running from something else. In the nightmare I turned completely (but kept running forward as you can in dreams) and there was Carla. But, it was Carla the femme fatal vampire of the black and white movie and she was naked with her huge breasts bouncing gloriously in the moonlight. Who said there was moonlight? She had long fangs and clawed hands and feet which did not seem to slow her down. I continued to run but also stay right by the couple who were now on the ground, entangled in some mortal struggle where Carla tore at Pete's neck with her fangs and claws, handing back pieces of flesh to little Frankie who stood looking at the whole scene with an angelic smile on his face, wearing my grandson's pyjamas. He too had fangs and while eating the chunks of flesh that Carla handed to him, gazed hungrily at my neck. Pete screamed silently. Then I ran into a skip someone had left in the road.

And woke up on the floor with Bruce tugging at the chain around my ankle and feeling as if my head had split open.

"You ok?" he said in a sleep-drugged voice.

"Yes." I managed to croak in what I hoped sounded like a normal tone. I was shaking and covered in cold sweat. Then there was a little mewl from the corridor and we both froze.

"Maaaama."

It was li'll Frankie.

Thankful for cover of darkness I struggled to my feet as did Bruce. I groped for the reading lamp at the other end of the sofa.

"It's ok Frankie. Come in the living room," I said in a voice that I hoped was loud enough for Frankie to hear but not loud enough to awake the lovers.

I took a quick look at myself in the living room mirror. I was just a blur of mad sticking up hair and staring, bleary eyes. I tried to smooth down my hair and look normal just as the door slowly opened and a barely conscious Frankie was framed in the door.

"Bad dreaaaam" he whined.

You and me both kid, I thought. Bruce was about to reach for the main light switch when I hissed at him,

"Don't. He's not fully awake; we're more likely to get him resettled if we just take him through."

So, Bruce didn't put on the light. I managed to pick Frankie up and hug him in and, feeing his body relax, I thought we were in with a good chance but just as we got into the corridor Bruce whispered that he needed a pee.

"Get the key." (me)

"Then I'll have to put the light on." (Bruce)

"Oh for god's sake. Just go." (Me)

"With you attached?"

I could tell his reluctance was tempered by also not wanting to awake the black and white movie horror parents.

"It's dark and anyway I've seen it all before." I hissed.

Nothing from Bruce. I was desperate now and almost too loud said,

"You big lummox, I'll stand outside the door, there is enough length on the chain."

"Well…"

"Hurryyyyy Uuuup." (Irritated stage whisper from me)

So that's what we did. Me, propped up against the wall just outside the bathroom cradling Frankie with Big Bruce weeing like a race horse. I was fairly sure Frankie was already back asleep. Then we changed places and I went while he held onto the limp Frankie. Then the three stooges, two of us chained, crept into the small bedroom trying to judge the outline of the bed and got Frankie into it. For some reason, possibly the fox, the neighbour's security light was on in the back and there was enough seepage through the curtains to create silhouettes. Just as I thought we were free and away a little arm got a half nelson around my neck. I lay part on, part off the single bed with Bruce standing at the end. Once I thought I felt Frankie relax I tried to move away but the arm cinched again. I knew from experience that this could go on for quite some time. Fortunately, with Bruce being in on the family mime act, I was able to indicate to him, even in the semi dark that he should make himself comfy at the end of the bed while allowing me to stretch out next to Frankie. I lay on top of the duvet and was in a much better, more sleep-friendly position than when I'd been on the sofa but this time I stayed brutally awake.

Bruce ended up laid out on the floor and there was no strain on the chain. I cannot remember being more tired but sleep just did not come.

Fear had almost worn itself out. I was like some listless herbivore, I thought to myself. Pete, sly and idiotic as he was, was a predator, in other words, a creature who takes his energy and life's requirements from other beings. Not all predators are lions and tigers and bears – oh no. Some are jackals or crocodiles, snakes and spiders.

But what of the prey? You see them. Rabbits. They will run like blazes if being pursued but once they think they are caught they just lie still and give in. stupid, stupid creatures. My daughter kept two rabbits. At least until the fox got one and we realised that the lid of the hutch needed weighting down in the wind. I told her no cat. I like cats but we'd had plenty and my days of carrying out headless mice and other presents, was over. We had one cat that, when it was pregnant, brought in two dressed trout it had clearly filched from someone's bar-b-q and yet another who once wrestled a not-quite-dead bird through the cat flap. Oh lord, the mess in the morning. No more. Plus you can't pretend to care about the world while feeding hundreds of pounds of meat to a pet every year. I'm just not that much of a hypocrite. So, having talked her out of a miniature goat, we got two rabbits. But wasn't that me now? Some bloody stupid prey animal waiting to die because I'd been cornered by a predator and his pack?

How did they know I wouldn't hurt Frankie? I had all the opportunity I needed right now. All they were concerned about was whether I'd escape until their plan b. had been put in operation. The thing is they did know. They may not have discussed it or even thought about it consciously but their subconscious had told them – him and Carla – I was not a threat to the child even though they were a threat to me. They had taken one look at me and knew - I was prey. Well, prey sometimes bites back but not the cub. I am capable of biting back, I know I am but not at a poppet like Frankie.

And what if I only drew the line at children? Did they care enough about Bruce to worry about me hurting him while he was asleep or did they just know it was not a possibility?

I could.

How?

I couldn't throttle him. No, my hands weren't big enough or strong enough.

Was there anything in the bedroom I could stab him with?

What?

A javelin you silly cow because let's face it a paper knife would just get you through the first layer of fat. And anyway – in case you hadn't remembered you are in a bedroom that is usually used for grandchildren and therefore devoid of anything that would hurt a fly (the insect).

Didn't Jason Bourne kill a bad guy with a pencil or a rolled up magazine?

I'm sure Bruce Willis killed someone by hanging them with a chain in *Die Hard*. You have access to a chain.

I hate it when you do that.

What?

Mix up actor's names with character's names when making comparisons.

Shut up. I'm trying to think.

Sorry.

There was that James Bond film where he kills the girl by painting her gold.

Oh boy.

But killing someone, although it happens accidentally all the time, surely isn't that easy. It takes the Irish cop ages to die in *The Untouchables* even though there is about a bath load of blood all over the house. In *Braveheart* Mell Gibson gives a great long speech while they are cutting his guts out.

You're doing it again...

In action movies it's always really easy to kill the peripheral bad guys. Presumably Bruce (Big Bruce not Bruce Willis) is a peripheral bad guy. It's the good guy who gets shot at all the way through the film by trained gunmen with highly sophisticated weapons who doesn't get scratched until near the end. In *Mission Impossible I – XI* or however many – they bring in bad guys by the truck load and they all die quickly and easily and sometimes gymnastically while TC / Nathan whatever, sprints off with his hair flowing in the wind.

And we've already established you are not Tom Cruise, you are a rabbit.

There are brave rabbits in *Watership Down*.

You are more *Peter Rabbit* and he is a scaredy cat.

Bugs Bunny?

He's not brave he's funny and clever.

I'd settle for that right now.

What are you going to do, joke your way out of this?

Then I thought I heard a sound. My ears felt as if they pricked up. Well, as we've recently established, I have a lot in common with a rabbit. It was not Bruce, who was now snoring more gently having gotten himself into a position which clearly suited him. Frankie was making mild whistling noises. It was not that. The coupling couple were silent. It was something else.

Oh please let it be the SAS. Please let them come storming through the window (without breaking more than one panel because I suspect it would take ages to reclaim for damages) and let them drag everyone off to prison or Social Services and send in cleaners to tidy my flat while allowing me to have a bath and a proper meal and a good cup of tea before needing to answer any questions.

No one came bursting through the window.

Maybe I'd imagined it. I was certainly tired enough to be hallucinating by now. Apparently you can audio hallucinate.

I may have drifted in and out of sleep, it's hard to tell. I had no idea of the time. It was that awful post-midnight place when bad thoughts come either in sleep or awake. It could have been anything from 1.30 to 3.30. I've not always been a great sleeper as I've said and if I woke in the night – having managed to actually get to sleep – and saw a too late to be awake and too early to get up time on the clock, I was sure I could feel the darkness pressing onto me. At that time of the morning it has an almost physical quality. And the dark does do things to folk. Bad stuff happens at night not at ten-o-clock in the day. Not so much accidents, they seem to be able to happen at any time. I'm talking about acts of cruel or evil intent which, of course is all nonsense because I got coshed in the morning. But one swallow doesn't make a summer as they say. They also say the exception proves the rule but if we get more side-tracked by silly sayings this story will never get cooked.

I could feel my mind spiralling off into more gobbledygook and I wanted to let it go all the way because sleep might follow and chloroform it but it wouldn't quite take me there.

So, having concluded I couldn't harm Frankie and it would not be physically possible to disable Bruce in any way that would benefit me, that only left any possibilities the new day might throw up.

Might Pete be in a charitable mood after a night of passion? Would Carla be able to persuade him to behave like the decent human being she deluded herself was just below the surface? Did she even want to? I'd fed Bruce like a 22 stone baby. Might he feel positively towards me? He certainly wouldn't stand up to Pete. Frankie had influence over Carla but no say in anything. I'd already gone over the possibility of Pete leaving me tied up but alive and concluded that I was now far too familiar with their faces, names and plans to let live. Maybe if the silly bugger had thought it through instead of bursting into my home prematurely he would have thought to wear a mask or put one on me.

Then I re-examined another terrible, terrible thought forensically. Forensics. I'd played with it earlier and pushed it away. None of them appeared to have taken any precautions regarding leaving biological evidence. I couldn't see Carla spending four hours cleaning down every surface, handle, cup, plate and spoon in the place and anyhow, we've all seen the films, you only need to leave one hair. I presumed and surmised that the failure of this enterprise meant they had to flee but maybe the plan always involved going abroad. Perhaps it was a plan they'd had to tweak because of the mess up. Perhaps this was the final job in a series of jobs. In films that's always the one that goes wrong.

I wished I could stop thinking about films and come up with an actual solution.

The reality was that whether this was plan a. or b. or even f. there was only one way to ensure that no evidence of a biological nature was left at the scene of a crime and that was to burn the place. Whether they left me alive or dead suddenly seemed immaterial. In fact being dead was starting to look like it might be of benefit. Maybe I could just die now of exhaustion and save everyone the trouble.

Why did I enter a competition for a scooter I didn't want and don't need? I probably wouldn't be able to give it away. My gran's monstrosity went from being stored in a plastic cover to the tip. But then we can ask ourselves these questions ad infinitum. There is never a suitable answer other than – you did – now get on with it.

I could feel myself drifting. Very quietly, without opening his eyes, Frankie said "Choo, chooh" and laughed. Bruce farted. I had a vague image of Bruce Willis in *Die Hard* reaching down behind his back for the guns to deal with Allan Rickman only this time the guns weren't there, just jars of beetroot. Then very vaguely and seemingly a long, long way away, I heard the noise again. The one I'd not been sure about before. Outside.

If I'd had to describe it I'd say it was the sound of someone trying to be quiet.

Chpt 14.

The morning after the night before

Go to bed with a headache, wake up with a headache. That is how the saying goes. And like a lot of other entrenched aphorisms it's often right and sometimes not.

A bird in the hand is worth two in the bush. What if the bird in your hand is a dead crow and the two in the bush are nice fat turkeys?

A stitch in time saves nine. Well, who mends things anymore? I do. Hence my minor income from selling discarded buggies – most of which need, as I've said, only a good clean anyhow. But I mean generally. When you can buy a T-shirt for £2.99 new – is anyone really going to stitch it when it gets a bit worn? Even though you can bet your bottom dollar, blood sweat and tears went into making it in that barricaded, fire-hazard cell they call a clothing factory somewhere in India or the Philippines. And – as the mood is going that way – there is no such thing as a *bottom dollar*. Money has become an illusion, as we can clearly see from the 2008 crash; there is always somewhere lower to go where money and morality are concerned.

It's a dog's life. That adage used to indicate a poor quality existence. How that one has changed. I recently saw a woman pick up a dog on a river walk because it arrived at a puddle! Pet food often smells better than what they serve in your local fast-food takeaway and grooming parlours and dog walking and dog day-care companies seem to be the only things growing in this economically precarious world. And, due to rising temperatures and over-heated homes and the ongoing 'humanising' of dogs, apparently the problem of dog flee-infested homes has gone up many 100s of %. Yum.

However, in this case, not only did I go to bed with a headache, I went to bed with a 20+ stone man chained to my ankle and I woke up with both. Not being a drinker (Methodist) I've never experienced the joys of a hangover but waking with a don't-come-near-me pain in the head and being chained to a smelly human walrus must come close.

I do occasionally have a sip of champagne at Christmas and have been known to indulge the same at a birthday which, many years ago now, led to my youngest daughter announcing in a group of adults – giving a very strange impression indeed – 'mummy only drinks champagne.'

What I needed now more than anything in the world was a very large mug of very strong tea. Sometimes nothing else will do. In the old days they used to give you a cup of tea and a slice of toast after you'd given birth. I mean before anything. Before taking you up to the ward or a bath or shower or anything. And let me tell you, there is nothing ever on this planet that tastes so absolutely fantastic. It could be the greyest tea, the limpest half done packet- white-bread toast but my word – mana from heaven couldn't replace it. That just goes to show, far from hunger being the best sauce, giving birth to a large baby and screaming the place down for a few hours and finally finding yourself relieved of a burden you've carried in the most ridiculous and uncomfortable way for nine months IS.

Usually the first thing I did in the morning was go for a pee but there was nothing there. Possibly I was dehydrated. But, also I'd been in the night. I remembered our little chain gang outing to the loo.

Wondering what the time could be I carefully peered around the room. It was still too dark to see clearly but not full dark with a little natural light managing to get through the rather thin curtains but at the time of year that could have meant anything from 4am to 7am. Then I remembered that as I was not in my own room there would be no bedside clock or other time telling device.

Just as I finished the slow, painful, head-torturing sweep of the room, a little hand patted my cheek. I turned back, causing a rip-roaring pain to chainsaw across my skull nearly making me puke. Quickly I sucked in breath and manged a weak smile when I saw Frankie's little eyes wide open and looking at me questioningly.

I carefully mouthed an eating motion. Frankie executed the family mime skills perfectly, shook his head and pointed down towards his pee machinery. I turned slowly again and, trying very hard not to let the movement reverberate up my body, yanked the leg with the chain on it. I had to do this three times before Bruce stirred. Bruce let out a long low fart and Frankie giggled. I concentrated on not vomiting and not letting my head explode.

Eventually Bruce sat up and stared around and then looked at us. Frankie was now also sitting up. He did the same motion to Bruce that he'd done to me, now grinning broadly at the novel situation and slowly Bruce nodded.

Why did we all conspire to silence? Well, I cannot answer for those two but for me it was simply that I did not want to know what was going to happen when Carla and Pete – or more specifically Pete - got up and the new day properly began. I just wanted a cup of tea and for my head to stop trying to radically change shape.

Bruce mimed a key. I pointed at Frankie. In this manner we established, through miming and pointing and facial expressions and nodding (I nodded as little as possible) and shaking that we would get Frankie to the loo pronto. Then we would go into the living room to retrieve the key to the extended ankle/hand cuffs. Then Bruce would pee. Then I could take a turn then we'd all go to the kitchen very quietly and have breakfast.

We retraced our little chain gang trip to the loo where Frankie peed for England. Once there I realised I did need to go. We chain ganged to the living room with Frankie in the middle holding the chain on his shoulder for us to limit noise. We were like three ghosts who had got very muddles up in a confusing afterlife. After a game of hunt the key we undid the cuffs, left the ghastly thing in the living room and went back to the bathroom. Bruce remembered to check that the front door was properly locked before he went into the loo and then I went in and somehow, we all ended up in the kitchen with the door quietly but firmly shut.

I noted the gun was still absent from the bench. I'm not sure why I thought it might have reappeared of its own accord but you can understand why I was a little obsessed with its whereabouts. I tried to tread carefully because at each footstep the gremlin on my shoulder whacked me in the skull with his sledgehammer. One great advantage of the Olympic headache was that it was almost impossible to form new thoughts.

There is a clock in the kitchen and it was saying 6.08am.

Bruce seated himself in the chair nearest the door and tried to look in charge. Frankie sat opposite and just looked expectant. I put the kettle on.

"Cocoa pops?" said Frankie hopefully.

"No dear. Porridge or toast or both?"

"Have you got red jam?"

"Yes."

The kettle was boiling and I managed a smile. Now I could see him properly, Frankie looked more tense than the previous day. Maybe he'd thought he'd wake up in his own bed somehow. Wherever that was. That happens to young children. Wherever they happen to be at night time, somehow, come morning, they are back in their own beds like magic. I remember nights out at the homes of other couples who had kids. The only way to have some sort of evening social life was to take the children and that only works if you are going somewhere where there are already children. We'd set off with promises of an early or at least reasonable return time. However, once there and the drink flowing and a free sober ride home for my husband, it never happened. In the early hours of many mornings I'd be driving home with a snoring man and sleeping children. Somehow I'd get them out of the car and into bed. In the morning they seemed non-the-wiser and never even noticed the absence of their dad as he slept off another hangover. I could get my middle daughter out of bed in the night and put her on the loo and she'd have no recollection in the morning. It must be nice to be so comfy and have so much trust in the person caring for you. But I did get the sense that Frankie knew about that trust and caring. He was far too well balanced not to. So what the *£$&%^> Carla was doing with Pete was any fool's guess. But this morning he was more watchful. Smart kid.

Moving carefully and trying not to jolt, I managed to procure a mug of tea for me and one for Bruce while the porridge cooked and I found some, thankfully, pre-sliced bread. I didn't think I was in a fit state to slice bread and anyhow, maybe I'd not be allowed to handle a sharp knife. I noticed the ones that I kept in a knife board on the bench top had disappeared. My dad's mum used to say if you sliced bread wonky you'd have a wonky life. But that's enough of silly sayings. I'm quite good at slicing bread but I don't think anyone's life was ever any wonkier than mine right then.

One way or another, things were going to wind up today. I felt the weight of lead in the pit of my stomach that somehow had eluded me yesterday. The nausea that the tea had been allaying, perhaps just with its inherent aura of calming normality, came back. The thing about yesterday was that there was still today (tomorrow). Now there wasn't. There was just now and that would only last until Carla and Pete got up.

I tried harder not to look at the door to the lean-to as I knew that would not help.

Putting a bowl of porridge in front of Frankie with toast and jam on a plate by the side, I asked Big Bruce what he'd like.

"It's a bit early for me." Which is something else interesting I've noticed. Big people often miss their breakfast.

Even though it was like eating blended concrete I managed a couple of spoonsful of porridge while Frankie scoffed his down and started chomping on the toast.

Bruce was looking around the kitchen and something about it seemed to make him uncomfortable. He obviously hadn't slept well but it was more than that. Maybe it was similar to his mum's or maybe he just had a bad feeling too. I certainly did.

"We'll be out of your hair soon," he mumbled.

It was such an oddly normal thing to say that I actually laughed, even though I paid a pain price. Frankie thinking things were taking a jolly turn laughed a little relief laugh. But Bruce went on.

"No, honestly. I know it's been tough on you but it's been tough on the boss too."

Surely Bruce wasn't trying for my sympathy?

"That prick at the warehouse messed it all up otherwise we wouldn't even be here." Was Bruce trying to convince himself or me?

I glanced down at Frankie who was making good headway with the toast and seemed unperturbed by the word prick. Bruce continued and I tried to put my face into a suitably receptive expression. With the pain I was in and the stress and lack of sleep or a shower, I may well have looked madder than a box of frogs, I've no way of knowing but if Bruce wanted to talk while I drank my cup of tea and lived a little longer that was fine with me.

"We should have been… well… a long way away by now."

Bruce's reticence to give details suggested one of two things. He really didn't think Pete was going to kill me or he'd never seen the many hundreds of films where the bad guy tells the good guy their plan because they are going to die anyway – so hey – why not waste a few moments in gloating – just before the good guy then escapes or another good guy with a bigger gun steps out incongruously from the shadows and holds up a tape recorder (ok – or more modern device) and waves it at the baddie in a neh neh neh neh way showing him he's been tricked. But what if the bad guy wasn't a smug idiot and just shot the good guy. Then, all the other good guy would have would be a recording of his mate getting shot.

Peter was going to kill me, I knew it with every fibre of my being and there was more fibre in me right now than a sack of bran. I was all straining fibres. Everything was on edge. My plan to get him to change his mind was the feeble brain child of desperation and tiredness and a knock on the head. But just then the pain was filling my head where thoughts should have been and, as I've already said, that wasn't a bad thing.

"Can I watch the inon ginant?" said Frankie.

For a moment I had no idea what he was talking about.

"Oh, yes. You finish your toast and we'll go and put the Iron Giant on the DVD player." I enunciated carefully hoping to save the need for more volume and ease the headache and nausea that were fighting for dominance.

"You don't have a land line do you."

It was a statement not a question from Bruce.

"No." I replied with very little interest in why he was establishing this point.

"Well, there you are. We've got your mobile. The boss will probs just smash that and lock you in or – you know – tie you up…"

He said it as if he were offering me a grocery voucher for the inconvenience of the last few hours the way Scottish Power offer you £25 'goodwill payment' when they've mucked you about for the umpteenth time and wasted hours and days of your life trying to get the most trivial customer problem fixed and I did not have the heart or the energy to call him a stupid idiot and point out that if I was Pete I would shoot me. For all the reasons I've previously stated. And, as for all the forensic evidence, I reckoned Bruce was going to be searching for some sort of flammable liquid before the morning was through. Thank goodness the upstairs neighbours were away. Having said that, we all have smoke alarms, so they'd probably have had time to get out anyway. I shuddered violently and had to breathe deeply again as a tsunami of nausea nearly overwhelmed me.

Then there was silence as Frankie gulped down the last of his jammy toast, Bruce finished his tea and I swallowed the last of mine with difficulty fighting the peristalsis that wanted to go in the wrong direction. But the ensuing silence lasted only about 3 seconds, which is longer than you might imagine, before we all heard the main bedroom door opening. Bruce straightened in his chair and experimented with a frown. I twitched nervously and felt dizzy. Then Bruce did a half roll of his eyes at me in what he possibly thought was a hopeful way but I looked down into my empty cup. Frankie fiddled with his spoon.

The kitchen door was pushed open and in stepped Pete looking around expectantly, cautiously. Maybe if you live the way he lived you always entered a room like that. He was just wearing jeans. No top, no shoes. The orange tan went all the way and it wasn't a pretty sight. I'm sure he thought he looked no end of a devil but in my view he was pigeon chested. Even though there was no one in the kitchen he needed to impress, he sucked up his chest.

Carla followed him in wearing my cotton bath robe and looking very dishevelled though still pretty even with most of her make-up smeared off.

Frankie ran around the side of the table furthest away from Pete and hugged his mum, thrusting his jammy face into her hip, smearing my bathrobe.

Pete hand signalled Bruce to take Frankie into the living room while not taking his eyes off me. I think this was meant to be intimidating but I just couldn't feel it. He looked so ridiculous. Just a pretend gangster. A pretend gangster with a real gun in the back of his jeans now that he turned to Carla but a pretend man nevertheless. It was as if someone had turned all my reactions off or switched them to a very strange, unreceptive frequency. I didn't feel I was responding to anything, even fear. When the big lummox and Frankie had exited, the love birds came into the room properly and shut the door.

"You ok?" That was Carla to me. Was she as stupid as Bruce? I didn't think so.

"Yes." I said because that was better than nodding in my current state. "Would you like some tea?"

"You got coffee?" asked Carla almost apologetically.

"Yes I have."

"Proper coffee?"

In response to that I went to the cupboard and reached up with my hand trying not to raise my head in case that tipped the pain and nausea scale in the wrong direction. And I held out the ground coffee bag for her to examine.

"Great thanks." She looked genuinely pleased.

"You?" I said looking sideways at Pete rather than turning my head fully.

"Green tea if you've got it."

And that was the nearest I came to laughing in his face and bringing my demise forward. I turned away too quickly, had to steady myself and breathe deeply then grabbed the canister containing the green tea while Carla sat down and Pete paced a little and looked out of the window by pulling the blind which had been drawn down – just slightly to the side. All it showed him was a greyish early morning light and an absence of activity. At this time of year it should have been clear and blue but no matter how hot it got it seemed to be overcast and this morning, from what I could glimpse, there were clouds. However, lack of activity clearly interested him more than the weather as he appeared to relax then came and sat at the table. In my head I was praying but not asking God to save me, not just then. I was begging please, please do not let Pete launch into one of his macho speeches – not without this shirt on. I couldn't bear it. I did not think I'd be doing my chances of surviving another hour any good if I started laughing like a hyena. Anyway – he was the hyena I was the rabbit.

But Pete did something much, much worse. He did something as bad as I could have anticipated.

Pete stood up and strolled over to the lean-to door and started fishing through the tangle of keys belonging to my various door and window locks that he'd shoved in his pocket.

I pivoted 180 degrees and although my head carried on spinning madly after the rest of me stopped, I somehow staid facing the sink and threw up into it. I kept on vomiting until I thought my legs must be empty. It went on and on. I filled the pot I'd cooked the porridge in and eventually slumped down onto the floor barley conscious.

Chpt 15.

Getting shot (the violence bit)

Carla managed to get me into the bathroom on legs of overboiled spaghetti. I was all headache now. I had headache in every atom of my being. Nothing else existed. I sat heavily onto the toilet seat that Carla hastily closed and just fell forward clammy; hot and cold at the same time. I tried to focus on breathing. Though you'd have to ask what the point was.

"Is ok. Is ok. You're just tired."

That was Carla from her perch on the edge of the bath. Even through the haze of nausea and the barbed wire of a ferocious skull pain I could tell she was practically picking out nursery furniture in her head. Boy did she sound pleased with herself.

I tried to say I'd be ok in a minute but I am fairly sure nothing coherent came out. I kept my eyes closed a little longer, drew in deeper longer breaths and then, extremely gingerly, sat up by putting my hands on my knees, pushing up gradually. Letting my head come up last like they tell you to in yoga classes. Of which I've only partaken on YouTube. I once tried a whole session when I found a young woman I liked and who didn't try to make the whole thing sound like the spiritual version of pink syrup but there was a lot of bending over and then up again and I actually made myself motion sick. Maybe I'm just a sicky kind of person.

Very carefully I opened my eyes. Even that hurt. I looked over at Carla and tried to smile. She wrinkled her nose at me in a 'there I told you so' expression. Really, who need ever utter a coherent sentence again after a day with this family? Then, on the basis that whatever is going on with you, however uncomfortable you are, however dreadful you look or feel, you know there are some people who would just much rather talk about themselves, I asked in a croaky, shaky, hardly-there voice,

"How did it go?"

There was absolutely no need whatsoever to ask what 'it' I was referring to.

"Grrrrreat. Duno if it's all the excitement (hell's teeth, that's one way to put it I thought) or just the change of setting but I did a lot of what you said and oh boy. Pete was perky if you know what I mean. I feel like I was real – you know – rrrreceptive."

This last word was delivered with such over emphasis and double/triple entendre I thought I might vomit again. In grimacing to hold back another wave, I hoped I was able to convert my rictus face into something approaching a conspiratorial smile. For all I know I may have looked as if I was trying not to pooh my pants but she didn't seem to mind.

I was more alert now and things had stopped swimming around, not least my own head. I tried to relax my shoulders which were up somewhere around my ears and everything was starting to go back into focus. I felt hollow. Hollow but definitely better. The headache was still there but the nausea was really on its way out – as it tends to just after you mega-puke. Good. Let's face it – you don't want to be feeling sick when you are about to get shot. How awful would that be?

"Come," beckoned Carla standing up more quickly than a woman in her condition should – by which I mean a woman wearing nothing but my bath robe, hence flashing her bits at me, "we go in the living room let the boys use the bathroom. When I get new house we're gonna have three bathrooms as well as an on-the-sweet in a big bedroom."

"How nice." I said standing up successfully and following curvaceous Carla at a shuffle not wanting to lift my feet too far off the floor in case I failed to remain earthed and went up in a puff of white smoke.

We made it to the living room, past the closed kitchen door where male voices could be heard, without further puke. My poor living room looked as if it had been hit by a tornado of teenagers. Bruce's bag lay open and he'd obviously had emergency provisions in there as well as the extra-long hand/ankle cuffs because there were opened packets of biscuits and what looked like packets of cheese and crisps and several cans of fizzy drinks. One, which was open but not finished had tipped open and left a dark patch on the carpet. The chain itself was in with the general mess. There were other people's clothes draped about and amidst it all Frankie sat on the floor looking into a smart phone which appeared to be playing a children's programme on its tiny screen sending coloured lights jittering over his face.

I sat on my sofa right in the middle of it all feeling disconnected. Frankie stayed on the floor with the phone and Carla fished around in the pocket of a jacket and got out the awful e-cigarette machine and started fiddling with it.

There was a kind of quiet that had nothing to do with no sound. It had more to do with stillness and anticipation. Everything seemed to be waiting and aware at the same time. I couldn't even hear what I regarded as morning noises from outside. Maybe the world has stopped turning in the night due to some apocalypse that we'd missed. Who knew, but the still silence was just there lurking like a lion in the bushes.

Then it happened. The thing the silence and everyone and everything else had been waiting for whether they knew it or not.

A door was unlocked. A door was opened. There was a pause. Then a man roared. Then a man screamed. Then a man threw and smashed things and swore and cursed and generally mixed himself up into an inhuman rage. Frankie went pale and dropped the phone and ran to his mother. She in turn dropped the e-cigarette and grabbed Frankie and waited to see just what the hell was going to burst through the living room door because as sure as eggs is eggs something was about to.

Bruce could be heard just repeating 'shit, shit. Oh boss, bloody hell. Shit, shit' and then what I had been waiting for more than anything else – Pete's voice.

"I am going to kill that flying black bitch right now. I am going to blow her flying head off."

I could not stand up. Carla could and she was standing back against the wall with Frankie now whimpering and clinging on to her as if his life depended on it – which maybe it did. She looked scared. I had no one to cling on to so I, unwittingly, gripped the sofa seat frame and braced as if I were on a fair ground ride. I never go on fairground rides. I do not like them, I never have. Bloody dangerous things.

The kitchen door crashed open – thud, thud, two strides was all it took – then the living room door ruptured, bounced and was shoved again and Pete, followed by Bruce burst into the room.

"Calm down boss, calm down, there'll be an explanation…"

Just how much of an idiot Bruce was I don't truly know but he was never going to get a job as hostage negotiator.

Pete ignored Carla and Frankie who had become a joint statue in the corner of the room playing an invisibility game but Bruce came in after Pete with Bruce waggling his arms like an annoyed school dinner lady waving a large ladle. Suddenly I felt hyper alert and not only could I feel Pete's animosity and Bruce's confusion, I could practically hear Carla mentally begging Bruce to get out of the way of the door so she could get Frankie out of the room but Bruce, stupid as he may have been, wasn't getting any closer to Pete than absolutely necessary.

Pete leaned right down and put his face in my face, spittle flying and he snarled like the rabid dog he truly was.

"I am going to blow your flying brains out if you've got any you stupid flying (then he said the C word, by which I do not mean Christmas)"

He stood up, brought up the gun which he had already retrieved from the back of his jeans and thrust it at me with great enthusiasm. Carla, seeing that she wasn't getting out of the room any time soon, decided to try to calm things.

"Baby, come on. Don't play with that. We'll sort this out. You scaring Frankie."

But without turning to her, Pete just spat out of the side of his mouth.

"Shut the fly up."

But Carla wasn't able to shut up.

"What did she do? I can't be that bad…"

But the look he gave her when he turned away from me and glared at her must have had something in it which suggested that whatever I'd done was as bad or worse than she could imagine because she clutched Frankie tighter, shut up and again flicked a glance over to the door as if in the hope that Bruce may have evaporated and cleared the doorway. And maybe the not being able to shut up thing was catching because before I could stop myself my mouth had opened.

"They think you aren't going to shoot me don't they but they are wrong. You are aren't you and you always were."

Now you may be surprised to know that even nutters like Pete don't like to think badly of themselves and the utter crap that came out next is just simple proof of that.

"I was going to try and find a way to leave you alive you stupid flying cow but not now. Now you've left me no choice."

"What I've done is given you every choice. What I've done is remove the reason for killing me." As I was saying that in a breathy voice with almost no volume, I knew it was pathetically wrong but it came out anyway. Then he did something to the gun with his thumb which made it click. Carla gasped, Frankie said "mumeeee" and Bruce sort of grunted in disbelief.

"Boss, don't do that," Bruce stammered in a high pitched voice. Then he looked at me sort of confused and panicked at the same time "It's not loaded. It's never been loaded. It's ok."

Then Pete stepped a little bit away from me and turned so that both Carla and Bruce could get a good look at the gun. His eyes seemed to be all pupil and popping out of his head and he had spit on his bottom lip and an unhealthy sheen to his skin. In what seemed like slow motion he raised the gun above his head and fired into the ceiling. Without the silencer, the blast was horrendous, plaster showered down, Carla flung herself back as if she wanted to get into the wall and Bruce threw himself onto the floor and crawled as close to the wall as he could get his great bulk. So, that answered one question at least. The gun was definitely loaded and Pete was the only one who'd known. Ok, that's two questions answered.

Then things sped up.

Pete grabbed a handful of my already untidy hair and with a great deal of energy, yanked me off the sofa. My whole body now pretty much had the coordination of a sack of potatoes, my ears were still ringing and I had plaster dust on me including in my eyes. He shifted his grip to my upper arm. The fact that Pete was so far gone that he clearly did not care one way or the other if any one heard was the scariest part.

He tugged and dragged and I stumbled and fell, once over Bruce's foot as we tumbled through the doorway into the hall. I was towed along, Pete's fingers digging into the flesh of my upper arm hard enough for the new pain to compete with the headache. Pete dragged me to the kitchen in this manner with me neither standing or crawling but a mixture of both until he dumped me unceremoniously in the doorway of the lean-to where the open boot of the scooter displayed the almost empty plastic container and the mess of powder around the bucket and the Belfast sink where the majority of it had been rinsed and swished away.

"What the fly did you DOOOOOOOOOOOOO?" This was an animalistic roar that is hard to describe. It was as if words were even more superfluous than usual with the head of the crime/mime family. Pete may as well have just grunted and growled and snarled and beat his chest. I got it.

This was the worst of all scenarios for him. Everything was gone. His chance to redeem a messed up situation. His opportunity for the home run and the easy life. Possibly his own safety. Who knew who he was answerable to. But most of all his manhood. He looked utterly, utterly stupid. And if you know anything about these types, the ones who are prepared to hurt others to get what they want and never think of the pain they cause or the damage , you will know just how thin skinned they often are.

"Carla, get our things." He screamed this towards the door. Then back at me. "We are leaving but first I am going to blow your flying brains out you stupid interfering old 'Christmas'."

He yanked me to my feet and propped me in the doorway. Why, I have no idea but he seemed to want me at eye level. He stepped back to get the shot. Again, why? I'm no weapons expert but surely point-blank is the shot to take if you want to be certain? I know, I sound like the mobster expert now.

Then, as they have a habit of doing, several things happened in close succession. Like if you spill the coffee you also drop the open milk carton and break a plate. Never just the one thing. On any given day you may stub your toe, walk into the corner of a table AND crack your head on a cupboard door. You lose your bus pass and your phone and your wallet (that one was my youngest daughter once in one afternoon.)

There was an almighty crash from the direction of the living room. I mean HUGE. It could have competed with the gun shot but it was a longer noise and marginally less alien. If I had to guess I'd have said it was my lovey Parker Knoll sofa hefted through the double glazing in the living room with a 22 stone man not far behind it. Then I heard Carla's panicked shriek and a long 'nooooo'. Then, more unexpectedly, little Frankie darted in through the doorway from the hall shouting in a high pitched, scared voice and crying at the same time,

"Don't hurt Grannie Annie. Don't hurt her."

Pete paid no attention. I was barely staying on my feet although why I was even trying to stay standing up-right is anyone's guess. I think I had ceased to think. All I know is that I experienced wild panicked horror as I became aware that lovely Frankie had joined our dreadful tableau.

I raised my eyes to Pete's face and saw nothing there. I mean nothing. His face was a blank and that is one of the most awful things I've ever seen. A human face devoid of humanity. It was like looking into a black hole. There was nothing there to appeal to, nothing to implore.

I turned my head a little and my eyes were inevitably drawn to the carnage in the lean-to. I had done quit a messy job it has to be said. I reckon only two or three seconds after opening the door it will have been entirely obvious to Pete what had gone on in there while I was locked in the day before and after he and Bruce laughed at me through the window and told me to pee in the sink. Everything was moving in a slow fuzz now as if wrapped in candyfloss. My head seemed to be made of candy floss.

I was vaguely aware of a shape, below hip level, moving fast across the kitchen towards Pete who only kept his mad eyes on me. Then Pete's face changed and he looked down without lowering the gun. Frankie had sunk his little teeth into the side of Pete's knee. You have to wonder who taught him this because I cannot think of any other place Frankie could have reached that would have made any impact on Pete right then. As it was I suspect the pain was not enough to have put Pete off what he intended to do but it certainly surprised him. And without hesitation he brought his free left hand down in an arced back swing that belted Frankie half way across the room where the poor little mite landed in a heap against the kitchen cupboard doors. Only thank god he didn't use the gun.

Just as Pete turned his attention fully back to me a raging ball of bleached blonde fury rocketed into the kitchen, screamed and launched herself at Pete. Carla appeared to my melting brain, exactly like the vampire girl of my nightmare, clawing at his face and neck and that, ladies and gentlemen, is when the second shot rang out.

It didn't so much explode from the gun as burst the air in the room, seeming to alter the nature of all the particles there. It was so loud. It was so contained. It was so everywhere at once. I could feel it in my ribs, spine and head. It blew my headache away. Then there was the silence of nothing. Not the nothing of a peaceful evening just nothing. Absolute. I could still see everything but in distant double and triple images. My vision first expanded and then began to reduce like in the old days when TV transmission had come to the end of an evening and the screen shut down to a dot in the middle only this seemed to happen by infinitesimal degrees in the new strange time/space relationship of my altered reality. Somehow I was facing into the lean-to. I could see dark wet splotches sprayed over the remains of the plastic that should have contained Pete's drugs.

As my vision reduced and reduced, my perspective on the lean-to changed. Instead of looking into the space I was angling slowly down. I looked past the scooter and its mess of crimson and white and plastic. I was looking at the wheels and they too were spattered. It looked like a very cheap horror film indeed with real looking blood but with everything else blurry around the edges.

Then the angle changed again and I was facing the concrete floor. Slowly, slowly it came closer and the little disc of my vision got smaller and smaller until it was nothing more than a tiny dot.

Then there was total black nothing.

Chpt 16.

Bus routes & fate

To say I would not have met these people during the ordinary course of a day is not exactly correct. I do not own a car so, when I'm not using Shanks's pony, I am on public transport. And there, let me tell you, is all life. At least here in Edinburgh, where bus fares are more than reasonable. I'm not talking about tourist season which runs from June to September and then again through Christmas and New Year. Christmas, obviously, starts a few weeks before Halloween, so not that long after September. During those frenetic periods you'd best be well informed of the pathways and tracks around the city centre that can get you from A-B avoiding the centre unless you want your ankles smashed by people who have lost the ability to travel anywhere without dragging those coffins on wheels behind them – and sometimes to the side as well. Somehow they also find a way to keep their smartphones in the air pointing at the various piles of stone or bricks that their friends are also viewing through a screen so that they can all go home never actually having seen anything. But yes – if not walking then its public transport.

It's not entirely true that all life is on the tram which is really for the tourists but definitely on the lovely buses you encounter all sorts. The drunk or drugged-up youth who decides to descend the steep narrow steps from the upper deck just as the driver slams on to avoid another tourist hauling two coffins and a smart phone who just stepped into the road without looking. You may find yourself seated next to someone who gave up washing during the Napoleonic era. You may be able to listen in to someone's loud account of who 'did' them last night or where they are going on holiday for the third time this year, who insulted them and is going to get what is coming or just exactly what they are going to tell the judge about this bitch or that cow or this bastard. Who needs telly? Not me.

I was once on the upper deck of the 100 which is the airport bus but you can use it even if you have not just got off a plane for a stag or hen do of puking and screeching and wandering around semi-clad or with desperate-to-be-original sayings printed across the fronts of T-shirts or hats. It's not my favourite bus for this reason but it was going my way. A young Irish man started the F'ing and as it was before 9am I just asked him please to stop. He said I could move if I didn't like it – so – red rag to this bull. I responded that I shouldn't have to inconvenience myself because a grown man didn't know how to behave on a bus at that time of the morning. He looked at his two mates for support but, sensible lads, they studiously ignored him. After further exchange, the best insult he could come up with was that I was behaving like a head teacher – yes, that really was the best he could manage – to which I retorted that he was behaving like a school boy so that was appropriate. He gave in obviously.

The no. 26 is my favourite bus in Edinburgh going as it does, all the way to Seaton Sands for just £1.70 although you have to be careful because there are two no. 26s. Why? I don't know ask Lothian buses. They go almost the same route until just at the end and then one version of this bus (sub headed Tranent) veers off just before you get to Seaton Sands. You then have to jump off while the driver smiles indulgently at you and tells you "it happens all the time". You jump on another bus back to where the original one veered off then jump off that one and get on a fourth bus by which time your fun and anticipation of seaside has left you and you are simply wondering – if it happens all the time, WHY DON'T THEY USE TWO DIFFERENT NUMBERS?

Frankie was different. I had a soft spot for Frankie immediately. I love children. And those chocolate button eyes and that curly hair and olive Italian skin and that smile… A block of granite would have turned to mush. Kids know if you are a push over. I am and he knew.

Carla was sort of a push over too. In a different way. Any woman that desperate to get pregnant gives very little of a damn about anything else. Even her psychotic partner's drug distribution problems gone awry thanks to Assonant 'amazon' Al couldn't hold her full attention. I can't say I didn't like her in some ways.

Big Bruce was easy to soften; he was already pretty much a pile of over-indulgence held together by heroic epidermis. With a stomach that size you didn't have to be a genius to know the route to that man's heart – or rather – first heart attack.

But Pete wanted to shoot someone. No adult gets a gun if they aren't a. prepared to - deep down and b. want to - maybe not so deep down.

Perhaps I sound like an expert but up until two days prior to my own personal environmental disaster, I'd never met Pete, Carla, Frankie or Bruce and I did not – to my knowledge – know anyone who owned a working fire arm. I'm fairly sure I did not know any drug dealers. Although one of my daughters knows an apparently respectable man who regularly takes cocaine and his wife is none the wiser. I suppose by current standards I've lived a socially sheltered life although I've had my share of knocks.

The thing is, someone was always going to get shot and it was always going to be me because I'm the person Pete wanted to shoot and he was the one with the gun. Some things in life are that straightforward.

Inadequate men (I know a few – so do you) need, more than anything, someone to blame when things go wrong. Because they are inadequate things often go wrong in their lives so they need a lot of folk to blame. The mental gymnastics required to shift the blame for one's own mistakes onto others, especially if those 'others' are complete strangers (me) who have not, cannot have had any impact on their lives, is extreme. That leads to extreme reactions on the part of said inadequate persons. It is a mental world of extremes. Just think of the racist. The wife beater. The child abuser who nevertheless sees himself as the victim. The corrupt leaders blaming minorities for what is wrong in their broken corrupt countries. And so on and so on. Pete was more small-time than any of those, maybe tiny-time but in the confines of my life and my even smaller flat, Pete loomed large.

The gap between when this started and The End – here in the kitchen with dark globules of blood on the floor, the encroaching darkness and the thunderous emptiness after the gun was fired for the second time - is like a lifetime and also a second. It's similar but not, to when you have a really good holiday and Time does that weird thing of making your normal life seem years away while the fun you're having is gone in a blink. But this wasn't a holiday. You might argue it was funny but it was not fun. And anyhow – funny is something you appreciate later, after the event has become a memory – and it doesn't look as if there is going to be a later. Right now I do not know where I've been shot but it cannot be good. My senses, like my earlier reactions, are all switched off or in the process of switching off and, frankly, after the events of the last 24 hours I'm ready for rest of any kind.

I was waiting for the pain and complete darkness and hoping oblivion came first. At the end, the little I could still see in the pinhole of remaining vision had brilliant stark clarity which did not match the numbness. Even the headache which must have been set in motion by the original pistol whipping seemed to have gone; blown away by the gun, like a hair of the dog curing a hangover.

And this account? Well, your life is supposed to flash before you when you are on the way out. I don't know about that and anyway – it's not my whole life. I didn't see Christmases from the 1960s or camping holidays in Wales or getting used to decimal currency or bonfire night in my Granny's garden. No. Just the mad capers of the previous twenty-four hours – give or take.

Chpt 17.

Breaking news

Hives Local Radio

'Staggering accounts have emerged regarding the harrowing ordeal of frail Edinburgh Grandmother Mrs Agnes De-Freitas. A neighbour who lives opposite the property where the elderly woman was tormented for many hours in her own home is with our reporter Dave. Dave, what has the neighbour over the road got to say about what she saw?

'Well Josie, it was as you say a harrowing ordeal for the elderly lady who is well known to locals and a pillar of the community. The neighbour, who does not want to be named says that she was home sick from work but managed to crawl out of bed when she heard what sounded like a car back firing. When she got to her window which faces the house where the harrowing ordeal took place she was just in time to see a sofa come through the window of the downstairs flat. She has not been inside Mrs De-Freitas' home but believes it to have been the sofa belonging to the elderly lady in question.'

'Wow – that's amazing. Is this sort of thing that normally happens in this area?'

'No, Josie, this is not the sort of thing that normally happens in this area. Neighbours describe this as being a quiet respectable area where very little happens.'

'Until now that is hey?' ha ha ha

'Ha ha ha, yes Josie.'

'On a more serious note Dave, was the neighbour able to see anything else after the sofa came out of the window? Any injuries?'

'Yes, Josie, the neighbour was able to see more, in fact she was quick thinking enough to video the following events and she posted some of it online until the police asked for her phone. But I believe a very large man fell out of the window after the sofa…'

'Ok, Dave, that's all we have time for at the moment but stay there and we'll come back to you after the commercial break…'

<u>Retro Radio 321</u>

'So, the usually calm suburbs of Edinburgh were disturbed just near Saughton Park today when police raided the home of Alma Freyer, a woman in her 90s who appears to have been the unlikely front woman for a terrifying gang of gun runners in this otherwise unremarkable part of Edinburgh. We'll bring you more on that after our next hit song *Oh What a Night* by Frankie Valli and The Four Seasons. Enjoy'

<u>The Edinburgh Bugle</u>

'An Edinburgh Grandmother was seen being rushed to hospital in the back of an ambulance as police surrounded a property in the Balgreen area of Edinburgh following police surveillance in the early hours of Tuesday morning after a tip off from a Polish man who lives upstairs but on the opposite side of the building. B said he became suspicious on returning from holiday and seeing firstly that Mrs Day's lights were on after 9pm. He said this is unheard of. He and his wife nevertheless tried to get up to their flat as quietly as possible with their sleeping daughter, thinking maybe the elderly neighbour had left the lights on accidentally and was in bed as usual before 9.

Later, however, he heard raised voices and went down to investigate. He said he did not recognise any of the voices and they sounded as if they were arguing. His wife insisted he call the police which he did, giving them the registration of a strange car parked outside the property in his space, one he'd not seen before and which meant he'd had to park further down the street. The police said that as it could not be classed as an emergency, in fact as it was difficult to classify the problem at all, they would send someone out in the morning to check on the situation. During the night however, an officer with time on his hands ran the registration number through the police systems and found a link to a notorious underworld criminal who they had been monitoring for some time. It was officers waiting to approach the building who were able to subdue the man attempting to flee the building via a downstairs window...'

'Love Local' news radio

Our reporters have been on the scene today of a horrifying drugs, terror, gang incident which occurred in the Murrayfield area of Edinburgh. Neighbours report an elderly woman being taken by ambulance in a lifeless state and covered in a great deal of blood. What were believed to be several gun shots were heard moments before a large man smashed a downstairs window with several items of furniture which he threw at waiting officers who had surrounded the building following high level intelligence that criminal fugitives were holed up in the property having taken the elderly Mrs Day-Freitas hostage. Mrs Day-Freitas is believed to be of Pakistani origin and it has not been ruled out that she may have, herself, been involved in terror activities and was drug laundering to raise funds for ISIS

The man who escaped through the window was brought down by four officers in riot gear and neighbours report seeing several armed police shouting at him to lie on the ground which he duly did. The man appeared to be shouting 'it's real' it's real' it's real' over and over again and those at the scene believed him to be under the influence of powerful narcotics. A small child was also taken away by ambulance but there was some confusion when the police attempted to arrest a female Polish neighbour instead of the Italian woman who said she was with the boy.

Breakfast News

Police are keeping tight-lipped about the events of yesterday morning in a quiet suburban street in Edinburgh near to Edinburgh Zoo. Police are withholding the names of all concerned until further investigations are concluded and until half a dozen or so videos filmed by neighbours and passers-by have been examined. Many of those who witnessed the incredible scenes unfolding were people leaving for work and parents taking their children to pre-school clubs. Everyone who was in the area has been offered counselling. We were able to get one piece of information from a man delivering to a neighbouring property later in the morning. He said that a man without his shirt on was hustled out of the property by police. They'd covered his head with what looked like a tea towel but he appeared to be wearing only a pair of jeans and when the towel momentarily slipped from his head there were what appeared to be scratches on his face, neck and chest which may have been made by an animal and one of his ears was badly torn.

The situation appears to be throwing up more questions than answers.

Over to the sport.'

1-o-clock news

The shocking news from Edinburgh about a drug den in the heart of the capital city, near to impressive local amenities and the famous Murrayfield stadium prove once again that drugs in Scotland will continue to claim lives at an alarming rate if nothing is done to stop the trend.

A spokesman for the government claimed there was no evidence to support the idea that significant cuts in rehabilitation services and support for those getting drawn into a life of drug dependency had led to the massive rise in drug deaths since 2011. The spokesperson was not able to give any reasons why he came to that conclusion.

In this case, the victim of the drug fuelled violence appears to have been a local grandmother. Her involvement with the gang remains a mystery but she is being guarded closely by police at

The Royal Victoria Infirmary. One of several eye witnesses said she was surprised the elderly lady was alive having been covered in so much blood. Mrs Day-de Freitas attends the local URC church even though she was a long standing Methodist. The local minister was shocked to find that she had any involvement with a drugs gang because she attended church events and seemed like a nice person but said the church would pray for her.

The Evening Chronicler

The Edinburgh underworld has not seen such distressing scenes since Burke and Hare according to the local SNP councillor for Balgreen June Evans. Mrs Evans who has been an SNP councillor since 1998 says she hopes people will understand this is not representative of Edinburgh. She pointed to the wonderful Saughton Park redevelopment just minutes away from the incident in question. 'It's a hugely popular area' stated the councillor 'No one need fear coming here. It's not The Bronx.' Questioned about the new train being set alight in the children's park, Councillor Evans said she hoped the press would not join in any negativity that may arise out of the unfortunate incident which, anyway – had 'not been fully explained.' She had no further comment.

It is understood that police investigations have led them to a local warehouse in the city and a number of further arrests have been made. Mention has also been made of a motorised scooter. It is not yet clear if this refers to a small motorbike or one of the motorised stand-on scooters that have been the scourge of paths and walkways throughout the city in recent months.

Three adults are believed to be in custody and a young child is in the care of social services.

6-o-clock news

Police have made a statement regarding the incident by Craiglockhart golf course in Edinburgh. We can bring that to you live now…

'With regard to the incidents which took place this morning in Stanton Grove Edinburgh we can confirm that three adults are under arrest and an elderly lady who is not regarded as a suspect is under observation at the Western General Hospital in Edinburgh. We'd ask anyone who has information which may be of use to the police in their investigations at this time to please come forward. Although we now have 14 pieces of video footage, if anyone has not as yet handed in film taken on their smart phones we would ask them to do so straight away. Thank you.'

9-o-clock news

Three Edinburgh MPs are travelling to Portugal to look at ways of tackling Scotland's drug problem. A cross party group of MPs are said to believe it would be helpful to also travel to Jamaica, Hawaii and possibly Malaga.

Random social media and online headlines

Tourist Mecca, home to Pensioner Drugs Pimp

Grannie Get your Gun

Serious Sofa Assault on Police

Polish-Italian Drugs Divas v Police in Bitch-slap incident.

Migrant gang assault British Granny

Is Edinburgh's mixed-race Drugs Granny related to Meghan Markle?

And because I wasn't dead and the male nurse on my ward on the third day of my very pleasant peaceful stay in a single room at The Western General needed money for repairs to his car, a reporter got into see me. I assumed he was a therapist. Everyone else seemed to have one. He had a note pad and said he wanted to ask me a few questions, was that ok? Still a bit blurry I had the chat. This is some of what I remember saying.

"I still can't believe what happened." (me)

"Hmmm. Yes. So tell me exactly what did happen." (Him, reporter/fake counsellor)

"You know what happened don't you?"

"Yes, of course but just recap in your own words. It's good for your mental health" (indulgent fake chuckle)

"Well, it's a bit of a blur but basically the scooter was full of drugs…"

There followed a long pause while he stared at me with what I assumed was the patience of the concerned Dr but he was actually willing me to fill him full of blood guts, violence and mayhem enough to keep his readership happy for five minutes on the commute to work. And because I'm me I went off on a tangent. And because he was, by omission, pretending to be a counsellor he couldn't really tell me to SHUT UP and get on with the story.

"It's just everywhere isn't it. What chance to young people have. They know the adults aren't in charge. The adults are too busy trying to have fulfilled lives or find themselves or work out how they can look like 20-year-olds as they approach 40. Or they are trying to hide debt from their partners or work out how to afford a better car than their neighbours. (He did look as if he was glazing over even at this relatively early point).

If you are a young working class or vulnerable person then someone like Pete is there waiting for you to get you hooked on something, anything that makes money for them. They don't care. If you are a middle class kid then the pharmaceutical companies take the role of Pete and they target you via your GP, your flying stupid over-protective controlling parents or your university councillor. Take a 13-year-old and tell her she has 'anxiety' issues and give her meds is much easier than dealing with her shit attitude – which is anyway – probably the result of the parent's controlling behaviour. Parents make children feel they are the centre of the universe and buy them everything so they think the world is theirs but they are not allowed any responsibility in that world. They aren't allowed to make their own decisions or fail at stuff. They aren't allowed to be told by anyone that they haven't made the grade. God forbid. The parents will be down at the school having the fight with whichever moron suggested to that child they weren't perfect. And when that child is well and truly fly'd the parents smooth that out for them as well by getting them medicated so they can go around telling the world they don't have arrested development or personality defects or lack of ability to just do things for themselves, they have 'anxiety'. And anyway – isn't having anxiety entirely normal in this world where being a gobshite gets you to the very top of the pile? We all need to get used to anxiety. Don't we? (At this point Mr counsellor/reporter appeared not to be writing anything on his pad but he wiped his forehead with the back of his index finger and glanced around the room as if looking for inspiration or the exit).

ADHD – don't get me started on that. Is there any wonder kids have ADHD (does it stand for - adults don't hug delinquents!) they are put in front of the equivalent of TV cocaine as soon as they can focus their eyes. (At the mention of cocaine he perked up and poised his pen but then it began to wilt as I continued). Once a kid's brain is whirring at that speed how is it going to slow down and their poor little bodies don't have chance to catch up because the furthest some of them walk in a day is from the front door to the car seat. They are always secured, controlled, restricted. 'Glued' to the telly. Strapped into the car seat. Harnessed into the buggy…"

Mr fake counsellor started looking around the room as if he were hoping a worm hole would open and suck him in but I was in my groove and couldn't stop.

"If the drug pushers and pharmaceutical companies can fund and funnel drugs into the human race so incredibly efficiently why can't we somehow get food, water, useful medication and education to where it's needed? Hey? Answer me that? Does that make sense to you? I mean where there is a will there is clearly a way" and on and on...

I'm not sure how long I went on in this vein or frankly what was in my own veins. They'd given me several things since I was delivered by ambulance to the hospital in a lot of excitement and confusion I might add. It may have been some very considerable time because at one point the counsellor/journalist closed his pad and glanced very ostentatiously at his watch. I was surprised to see such a young man wearing a watch. Everyone seems to rely on their phones to tell the time. Well to tell them everything in fact. How far they've walked, what they should eat/wear/think. Anyway, the journalist-counsellor was beginning to loosen his tie, clear his throat and rub the top of his leg with the palm of his, now pen free hand when the door opened smartly and a fierce looking ward nurse marched in, glared at the journo-counsellor with her hands punched into her hips. He stood up very quickly knocking over his chair. Without saying anything she pointed a solid finger attached to an even more solid arm at the door. Mr journo-counsellor exited more smartly than the door had been opened – even gratefully. And without saying anything to me the mime nurse marched out after him. Maybe she was related to Pete, Carla, Bruce and Frankie.

What appeared in *New City News* the next day was this –

'One of our investigative reporters was able to gain exclusive access to the Edinburgh Grandmother at the centre of the violent gang related disturbance which rocked a quiet suburban neighbourhood in the city a few nights ago.

Frail, elderly Ms Anne Day-de-Freitas was being kept under observation and little is known about her medical condition though she was understandably confused. It is believed she suffered at the hands of a known drugs cartel in her own home for a number of hours when a local narcotics dealer used her flat to hide a stash of cocaine believed to have a street value of many hundreds of thousands of pounds.

Unfortunately, Anne was unable to give any clear indications of what happened as she was rambling incoherently – clearly suffering from PTSD. We can only hope she will be given the care and medication she needs. We will bring you further information as it becomes available.'

Fortunately, once mime nurse had ejected that sneaky little sod, no one other than nurses, doctors, the lady with the tea trolley and the auxiliaries with my meals entered again until it was time for me to get my lazy backside out of that bed and go home. They say you don't sleep in hospital. I don't know. I slept like the proverbial log. I slept like the dead. I slept for England.

But if you can hang on just a little while longer I will tell you what actually happened in the lean-to/not-a-garage/sort-of-conservatory. Briefly, because I'm not one to ramble but I think you deserve to have some sort of clear explanation. The main thing you need to know at this point is that the blood was not blood it was beetroot because stupid Pete shot a jar of pickled beetroot instead of me.

Chpt 18.

What actually happened

You already know most of anything that is worth knowing about this torrid tale, this sorry story, this freaky fable. But let's imagine it's an episode of *Columbo*. You don't need a narrative to be all surprises and revelations to enjoy it. And frankly, unless you've led a very restricted life you will begin to recognise certain patterns in literary or cinematic offerings which mean you can work out a lot of what is going to happen, or has happened, by elements that have nothing to do with the unfolding events.

Some of us will work out, just by reading the screen credits, who is going to be alive at the end of an action film for example. And of course if it's one of those moronic super-hero franchises you know most of the main characters need to survive because there is merchandise to sell and they haven't as yet just started putting random actors into those ridiculous costumes safe in the knowledge that no one will notice or care. So, during a film it's not so much about how things will turn out but how character x or y is going to remain alive in the tangle of strangely contorted difficulties a desperate film writer has concocted.

The thing I love about *Columbo* is that they go heavy on the dramatic irony. The audience is let in on everything right at the start; it is dished up on a silver platter by a very willing waiter with a smile and a conspiratorial wink. In some episodes the act(s) of murder is (are) complex and extended and take up quite a proportion of the screen time. Also, we never doubt that Lt Columbo is going to outwit the villain every single time. In some cases we knew that he knew from the first introduction just by the shake of hand with a give-away-heavy signet ring or a badly executed fake reaction to grief or a failure to be surprised by something that would have confounded an innocent person. So it's not even as if we are waiting for Lt Columbo to work it out. So why then was it (is it) one of the best detective series of all time? Well, those are easy questions. Peter Faulk was a darling. He could act. He could deliver a line. He could improvise. He could hold our attention even if he wasn't saying or doing anything. The stories – certainly in the early episodes - were brilliant and the scripts were to die for and peppered with great humour much enhanced by the man himself. What we watched for was the fun, the triumph of good over evil, often in very pedestrian ways, and – though Faulk himself denied this – the triumph of the little ordinary working class guy 'on a cop's salary' over the wealthy, arrogant bigshot who thought himself invincible/ untouchable.

So why – I can hear you ask impatiently – are you making this great long comparison with *Columbo*? You are not a little Italian-American or a cop and this is not a detective film and nor is it the 1970s blah blah blah. Only because I am going to fill in some gaps and that is something Lt Columbo always did and something I always enjoyed.

One such gap you may be interested in although you have guessed, you want to be proved correct – is what happened in the lean-to.

Well the very bad idea I had was very bad indeed. Like the girl with the curl. *'When she was good she was very, very good but when she was bad she was wicked'*. The bad idea was worse than awful.

You have to factor in, if you are judging me, that I was locked in my own lean-to / garage / shed and I was a bit battered, bruised, very tired and in shock and to add insult to injury the two stupid blockheads thought it was hilarious to leave me to pee in the sink. Which I did not. I used the bucket, remember.

I got to thinking not just about all the misery that drugs cause but how this particular situation was driven entirely by Pete's need to find a solution to the exact, actual, specific drugs in the scooter. You can tell I'm getting agitated again at this point even in recollection because I don't usually indulge in tautology.

My brain wasn't working at its best and I was just frantically thinking how to resolve the situation without anyone, especially little Frankie or me, getting hurt.

'Remove the reason for them all being here' was my brain's rejoinder; the great solution and boy did it seem like a good idea right then. I think the sensation was akin to when you are very young and you have an idea that you are sure no one has ever had before or think of a potential solution to some problem that humanity has hitherto thought insurmountable. And you feel that way because you are too young to know that almost no thoughts have not been thought before and most apparently insurmountable problems are a. man-made b. very easily solved. It is finding the will to resolve things that is the biggest most human blockage of all.

I digress.

After Pete and Bruce had gone back down the side of the building to leave me to pee without a toilet and after I had done so, my bad idea started to walk on its own two legs and march around. Then it started strutting and posturing and I was so impressed, I became a fan and followed it to its conclusion.

I manged to find a garden fork and a garden trowel. The packet was wedged so tightly into the trunk I daren't risk trying to get it out so I stabbed the package with the gardening fork and then worked the tines up and down like one of those old can openers, until there was a big enough hole to get the trowel in.

I had been going to start trowelling the stuff one tiny trowel load at a time down the sink with the tap running but I'm not entirely stupid – though you may beg to differ. I did not want the air full of drug dust and me in a confined space breathing it all in. I half-filled the bucket with water while leaving the tap running but not full-on and ladled the powder into the water in the bucket to damp everything down. Then I swilled the contents down the nice large Belfast sink. Just getting rid of the stuff in the boot seemed to take forever though I suspect I was working quite quickly, in somewhat of a fever brought on by the situation and a highly motivating sense that I was doing something to make things better. Plus of course, there was the worry that I might get caught in the act. The plan would only work, I had concluded, if by the time it was discovered, the powder was all gone. Discovery midway would solve nothing and possibly hasten my violent end. My heart was drumming, I can tell you.

Once that was gone I was emboldened to do the same with the stuff under the seat as the two wayward young men seemed quite happy doing what they were doing outside thinking they had got one over on a silly old woman. I think this notion spurred me on even more. Something was spurring me on. I was beginning to think that it was not just a good idea but a bloody brilliant idea.

There were two packages under the seat but they were not as tightly rammed in as the large one in the boot so I was able to take them one at a time, slit them and dispose of them directly down the sink which was much quicker.

Once it was all gone I spent ages rinsing the sink down and the bucket and wiping the outside of the scooter and the floor area with a damp rag I'd found. A damp rag I might add accompanied by a very large spider. On this occasion I was not as bothered as I would have expected to be. I presume I had bigger fish to fry – or cocaine to flush. Anyway – there was still an awful mess and I don't know why I bothered.

When it was all done, I washed my hands again and again with the cold water until they began to ache and I had to hold them under my armpits to get the feeling back. It was some time before they were comfortable and by then it was really quite unpleasantly dark in the lean-to but I still did not want to pop on the light. I just felt I did not want to view clearly what I had done. Maybe I was already beginning to have doubts about the efficacy of the plan and the possible consequences.

As for the drugs having a street value of hundreds of thousands of pounds as per the news reports, a nice young police woman I spoke to in the hospital said this was wildly exaggerated. Prices had dropped considerably. What was stashed in the scooter – even with the small amount I'd not found – was nearer to eighty or ninety thousand pounds worth. But it was the final load in a series of deliveries this particular group were making prior to going to ground as things had already got hot for them. And Carla's plan of going away somewhere was really in the pipelines.

I was surprisingly cold on what was not a cold day and exhausted by the time I'd finished and very glad to be released from my dungeonesque confinement. I had, and you will find this very difficult to believe, contemplated telling the unwelcome houseguests of my actions as soon as they let me out. In my strange confused state locked away I'd imagined somehow that they'd be angry, Pete would be furious, but they would up sticks and say – oh well, no need to stay any longer – and just go.

As soon as the door opened and I stumbled a little blinded by emerging from the darkness to the sudden light, into my own kitchen, I was horrified at what I'd done. Good lord had I forgotten the gun? Had I forgotten that Pete was an unstable idiot with a gangster fantasy and very little self-control? Had I forgotten that his opening welcome had been a gun butt to the forehead? Had I forgotten that there were three adults, none of whom I'd be inviting for tea any time soon, who all currently had more say-so in my home than I did? Was I mad? Don't answer that.

And it could have all ended there. As I was let into the kitchen, only one of them, any one of them, need have stepped into the lean-to/garage/not conservatory and that would have been the end of it and not in any of the ways my earlier silly fantasy anticipated. But they just didn't.

And so I began to feel incredibly sick. That was the start of the real headache and the dreadful nausea and the rising panic every time anyone went anywhere near the door.

If I could have done it, I'd have dredged every grain of that monstrous stuff up out of the drain into the sink and put it back. All I could think of is – he'll kill me, he'll kill me when he finds out. And not in a humane way. 'Humane' by that point had come to mean, 'quick and efficient' i.e. a single bullet to the head rather than a one way ticket and 7,000 Swiss francs for Dignitas. As I've said previously, your parameters can change quite significantly depending on circumstances. Now I envisioned torture and beatings, rage and so on. Every mafia movie you've ever seen but without the thrilling accompanying film score.

As it happened, and as you know, the empty scooter was not discovered that night and who knows, perhaps the extra few hours bonding with Frankie and softening the already pudgy Bruce and the hard-faced Carla, really may have altered the outcome just a scintilla in my favour. Just enough for the angle of the gun to be just enough off.

Frankie and I were getting along famously anyway. He got the hang fairly quickly that his little sojourn in the strange flat was quite pleasant – as far as it could be with a lunatic stepfather a gullible mother and an 'uncle' figure who had no more brain development than Frankie himself. But, if I'm not mistaken, any malign intent on Bruce's part or even willingness to do his master's bidding was somewhat reduced by the following morning after a number of very filling meals and some human interaction.

Frankie loved the toys, the food, and generally was having as nice a time as he'd have had anywhere. And he'd certainly worked out that if he wanted any of the creature comforts of life in a hurry, Granny Annie was the go-to gal.

So, Pete discovered the stash was missing, gone, cleaned out, disappeared, flushed, never to be recovered on the second morning. Maybe he was even more irate because having, as he thought, got out of the first fix, the idea that it had now all been for nothing was harder for his ego to stand. Or he was in hoc to people even worse than himself. A very strong possibility. Plus, the idea of having to explain that the old cow they'd held hostage while plan b. was coming to fruition had flushed the stash while he and Bruce were smugly smoking, was just too awful for the macho world he inhabited.

He'd been made a fool of as well as losing his considerable chance to make a lot of money out of other people's misery and skip off to wherever he intended to take some R&R.

To say Pete was raging doesn't really quite cover it. Also, rage suggests to me a beast of some proportions. Pete was more like an hysterical 13-year-old girl but in a man's body, with a tan, wearing only jeans and totting a firearm.

So, yes, I was dragged to the kitchen door and made to look at my misdemeanour like a puppy being made to look at its poop in the corner or a child being made to look in the mirror at the chocolate stains around his mouth while he is still denying that he was the culprit who ate his sister's Easter eggs.

Fear is an awful thing. Sound alters. It becomes hard to breathe. You are supposed to have a fight or flight mechanism that kicks in but after the debilitating, exhausting time I'd had, all that was left was the feeling that my body was made of lumpy, coagulating custard. I had no idea how I stayed upright. It certainly felt as if it was nothing to do with me. Yes, I know I said potatoes earlier. Well potatoes in custard in a bag.

The police were not convinced, I could tell, that Carla and Bruce were unaware of the full-and-ready-to-fire nature of the hand gun but I am convinced. I was there and saw their faces and reaction when Pete fired the first shot. I am not Lt Columbo but you don't need to be the great detective to have seen the astonishment on Carla's face, the sheer bloody panic on Bruce's. And he did heave my Parker Knoll sofa through the window, smashing the pane to smithereens (and I still don't know what they are) walloping one poor copper on the shoulder and showering another in glass. He was so beside himself was poor Bruce, he failed to notice the police van or the officers in very close proximity to the house as he lumbered down the path out onto the road where he was still running with two police men attached to him and it was falling over his own feet that finally brought him to the ground in the middle of the road. Quite a few of the amateur film-makers got that one on their smartphones. Bruce was quite famous for three days.

Carla was scrambling to get her bag and make her own escape when Frankie managed to get out of her clutches and follow Pete and me into the kitchen and that is where he made the knee-high assault on his stepfather and where that horrible man swiped the poor little mite across the room. Of all the things that happened that was the worst. For that I hope Pete rots in hell. It was also the final straw for Pete. He turned his awful, dead-eyed gaze back to me and even in my disconnected state I could see nothing. By which I mean nothing in his face that indicated he had any human feeling left. Nothing at all. I think hatred or extreme fury does that. It wipes out the humanity. And a nanosecond before he pulled the trigger and that deafening explosion altered the world right in my face, Carla launched herself at him.

Roll back just a couple of seconds or so and she, having realised Frankie was away, darted to the kitchen to apprehend the boy and was in time to see the back-hander. Then, just like the vampire in the dream, she hurled herself at Pete with an agility I would not have foreseen and her weight pushed the gun off target just before she started clawing his face and sank her teeth into his shoulder while scratching down his nose and chin with her other hand. He dropped the gun after he'd shot the beetroot but she did not stop. She was WILD.

The bullet smashed that largest jar of pickled beetroot but by then I was already in the act of crumpling unhurriedly onto the floor like a forgotten Christmas decoration in February, without in anyway being able to stop myself even by putting out my hands. I just fell. Very slowly, as I recall. I fell and fell and I could already see the splatters of crimson juice everywhere but I have no memory of the smell of vinegar. But then I have no memory of the screaming harpy that was Carla seeking, like a black widow spider, to feast on her mate. And that was another thing the police woman told me. Subduing Carla was more difficult than controlling either Pete or Bruce.

After dragging me to the kitchen – and I'm no bird-skeleton little old lady, walloping Frankie, firing the gun a second time and being set-upon by the wrath of Carla, Pete seemed to go into shock himself. It was the police who managed to prize Carla off or it may have been hearing Frankie once he'd recovered enough to start crying. Pete said very little after that apparently.

Like everyone else, the police thought I was dead and when they realised I was alive there was a mad panic to get a medic and find out where all the blood was coming from. Silly buggers. They must have been able to smell the vinegar.

I wasn't even entirely unconscious and by the time they had removed Pete, Carla and Frankie. I began to smell the vinegar. My senses came back to me gradually. And I could tell by the way Frankie was crying further and further away that although he was hurt he was not badly hurt and at that point I decided to give in and let things take their course. I did not want to talk to anyone and I did not want to deal with anyone so I closed my eyes and, after doing a quick inventory of my body to see if any bits hurt more than they should or more than could be accounted for by age or the exertions of the last few hours or by ending up on the floor without having done anything to break my fall, I checked out and decided I'd not respond to anyone for a while.

The last thing I saw clearly as I let my eyes slowly close was the shiny glint of the metal on the underside of the maroon scooter as if it were winking at me.

Epilogue

Carla got a suspended sentence and Frankie back and Frankie now has a baby sister.

Bruce had to have hospital treatment for cuts and bruises and he got some time in prison for serious charges although his sentence was commuted on the mitigating circumstance of him basically being an idiot. Having become a vegetarian and a born again health fanatic, he lost 8 stone and, from prison, became a bit of an online celebrity for the second time as felon slimmer of the year.

Carla managed to avoid prison by pleading coercion. I may or may not have helped her in this but I did emphasise that I thought she could be a fit mother and with a bit of help could be a good one.

I got a new sofa and my window repaired. My youngest daughter arranged for my flat to be cleaned to within an inch of its life. And let me tell you, cleaning up beetroot is no mean feat along with glass and food debris and cocaine residue. Once home, I went shopping and stocked up with all my favourite groceries (Bruce's rubbish had been ejected by the cleaners) and barricaded myself in until the most hardy of door-stepping reporters gave up.

Frankie, who had a right shiner on his cute face from the back hander that Pete dealt him, is fine and living in a nice flat with his mum and new baby. He is on the 'at risk' register and gets visits from social services and monitored at school where, I believe, he is doing well.

That pretty much ends our tale of beetroot and barbarism, sex and self-worth, drugs and destiny. Have a lovely day and I will hopefully see you for the next story.

Oh, yes. Pete got a long stretch in prison for all the drugs stuff and attempted murder and other charges, some I'd never heard of. He deserved it all. There were two things he was not charged with but should have been; being an appalling role model for a young child and being a flying moron.

The End

❧

70's Summer Montage

Heady musk of August heat
Happy dirt-peppered roving feet
Deaf to Time's tenacious beat
Desires just to eat play eat
Bent metal folding tartan seat
Back of Dad's bike nothing yet to delete

Camping out in Wales on crisp grass baked biscuit brown
Lard fried egg sandwich limp bread sunny yolk drips down
Square greying photo of me toasted face book frown

My funny fish pale dad with emerging beer pot
Carries clingy brown girl to sea-cold from sand-hot
No toes below the surface where they may get got

Loud West Indian wedding young bride in stiff white
Sulking in blue bridesmaid's dress reggae thrums the night
My sister got the pink though I put up a fight

If you come in again you stay in mum's beige threat
Sunday's with English granny skinned knees mud pies all wet
Condensed milk sweet lemon cake cram what you can get

Caribbean smooth yellow cornmeal no grey oats
Wardrobes with sharp shoes spangled frocks dusty fur coats
Dip in big red curry pot if you want some goats

Khaki newts mauve butterflies tan and orange walls
Mums in kaftans A-line skirts skipping ropes bats balls
Out 'til dark pretend not to hear dad when he calls

Tarmac melts toffee-made world as the dream dissolves
Heat ripples rise distorting as the day revolves
Summers chill winters lengthen innocence evolves

Merging days endless joy ice-cream jingle tongue cool
Gardens are our kingdom a piece of glass a jewel
Ignorant bliss no painful perception childish lucky child-fool

by Amanda Baker

(adapted from the original version in *Other Stuff* 2013)

Also by Amanda Baker

Adult novels

The Companion Contract

Eating the Vinyl

Anthologies that include Amanda's work

The Iron book of New Humorous Verse (poetry anthology)

ROOT (short stories)

Dystopian novella

Zero One Zero Two

Epic environmental poetry story

Casey & the Surfmen

(also available as an audio story on bandcamp)

Adventure trilogy (8 – 12yrs) STARRING A GIRL

bk1. *Eleanor & Dread Mortensa*

bk2. *Eleanor the Dragon Witch & the Time Twisting Mirror*

bk3. *Eleanor & the Dragon Runt*

Picture book in verse for little readers
Ella & the Knot Fairies

Sort of autobiography
Maybe I'm not a Pigeon

Solo poetry anthologies
Other Stuff
Humorous Verse for Parents

Printed in Poland
by Amazon Fulfillment
Poland Sp. z o.o., Wrocław